Breakfast with Santa

by

Carol Henry

The Lobster Cove Series

Breakfast with Santa

Cover Art by *Debbie Taylor*

The Wild Rose Press, Inc.
PO Box 708
Adams Basin, NY 14410-0708
Visit us at www.thewildrosepress.com

Publishing History
First Champagne Rose Edition, 2015
Print ISBN 978-1-5092-0442-7
Digital ISBN 978-1-5092-0443-4

The Lobster Cove Series
Published in the United States of America

Dedication

To my own High School Sweetheart with all my love.

His long, lingering kiss

threw her into a tailspin of remembered passions. Before she could wrap her arms around his neck and sink into his embrace, he let her go.

Stunned, Katelyn could only stare as a hot, searing heat of embarrassment washed over her.

"I've wanted to do that since you walked in the lodge dining room wearing that sexy elf outfit last Sunday. I know you're engaged, but I'm not going to apologize for that kiss. This has been the best homecoming I've ever had. Thank you, Katie, for letting us come into your home."

Oh, my God! This was her worst nightmare. "That *was* you! You *were* the one who played Sant—oops!" She looked at Kurtis, hoping he hadn't figured out what she had been about to disclose. "Why didn't you say something? You kept staring at me all morning—I looked like a freak in that get-up."

"Definitely not a freak. I'm sure you turned a few heads, including mine. It was hard to concentrate on the kids with you in the room. You have a unique flair with kids, by the way."

"Up, up," Kurtis cried, his arms flung out to his father before Katelyn could respond. Mark lifted him into his arms, gave Katelyn a quick peck on the cheek, and turned to leave.

"Me kiss Katie."

Kurtis leaned toward Katelyn. If Kurtis caused her heart to melt any more, there would be nothing left but a puddle in the middle of the floor.

Praise for Carol Henry

JUELLE'S LEGACY – voted #5 Best Romance Novel,
Preditors & Editors Readers' Poll 2014

"This [story]…warmed my heart. Juelle…faces multiple layers of devastating secrets…She stands up for what is right…makes the lives of others better…is humble yet strong. Hunter McClintock…a war Veteran…adds iron strength, a loyal character, and a great deal of sex appeal to little Lobster Cove!"

~Nicci Carrera, Author

~*~

NOTHING SHORT OF A MIRACLE
voted #5 Best Romance Novel
Preditors & Editors Readers' Poll 2013

"Carol Henry is a gifted writer who paints you a picture of all the fine details of the season. A master at pacing…The story is like a warm hug."

~W.A. Darling, 25 Days of Christmas Stories Review

~*~

SHANGHAI CONNECTION
voted #2 Best Romance Novel
Preditors & Editors Readers' Poll 2012

"Rich with setting and suspense…Carol Henry brings the setting alive with lush, vivid descriptions…and keeps you turning pages until the very end"

~Alicia Dean, romantic suspense author

~*~

"Carol Henry's beautifully written descriptions immerse you in the surroundings where there are plenty of edge-of-the-seat thrills…a connection you want to make!"

~Mal Olson, author of adrenaline-kicked romantic suspense

Chapter One

Gads! How did she ever let her father talk her into playing an elf for his lodge's breakfast with Santa? Dressing like a tiny elf at her age was just going outside her comfort zone.

Katelyn Sullivan sat at her old dressing table at her mother's house. She leaned in toward the mirror and applied the final touches of heavy makeup. Santa's elves needed to be bright, colorful, and chipper at Christmastime. And this was a well-attended, annual occasion the Lobster Cove Lodge put on the first Sunday in December. Breakfast with Santa was one of the big hits of the season. She sighed, leaned in closer to the mirror to check for flaws. The big splash of deep rose-tinted rouge was perfect. She'd lined her eyes in black, and swiped her lashes with a darker shade of mascara, which made them look two times longer than they really were. Her hair was too thick for a ponytail, so she wound it up into a top-knot and plopped the green felt elf cap on top of her head. *Great!* The ridiculous outfit with red tights they had given her to wear made her legs look too long and too skinny. She tugged at the hemline. Thankfully, the tights covered her bottom sufficiently, because the green skirt was so short there was no bending over without revealing everything. The tassels on her pointed olive colored shoes were also a joke. Her five-five stature was simply too tall to pull it off. She was definitely going outside her comfort zone, even though it was for a worthy cause.

Way outside that particular comfort zone.

It was a good thing her fiancé, Sven Olson, had flown to Norway with his parents to attend his grandparent's fiftieth wedding anniversary celebration. He wouldn't see her dressed like a ridiculous grown elf that looked more like a circus clown. She could only imagine his reactions, not being one who liked to draw attention to himself. She crossed her fingers no one would snap pictures of her and show them to him when he returned. She'd be mortified. It was one thing to entertain the kids in the community, another to be ridiculed by her fiancé.

"Gads! I do look more like a twenty-six-year-old clown," Katelyn told the elf staring back in the mirror. She sighed, hung her head, twirled around on her toes, and headed out the door. If her mother laughed just once, she was going to run back upstairs and hide in her childhood closet for the rest of the day—she didn't care how childish she acted.

"Oh, Katelyn, honey. Don't you look cute? The children will love you dressed in that adorable costume. Why, I bet you'll be the best dressed elf there."

Her mother's words didn't appease her doubts one bit. She didn't look cute. She certainly wouldn't have used the word adorable to describe this getup.

"I look like a moron at one of those old-time carnivals where everyone pays to peek at the freak."

"You do not. Honey, you'll have fun with the kids, as usual, and before you know it, you'll forget you're dressed as an elf."

"How do you know? Did Dad ever make you dress like an elf?"

"That's beside the point, my dear." Her mother waved her hands in the air, then reached for Katelyn's arm and dragged her toward the kitchen. "Now, listen. I've made two blueberry pies for the pie sale. Be sure to give them to Mrs. Rauch. She'll need to price them along with the other pies. This is always the lodge's auxiliary's biggest sale of the year. I've put them in the pie carrier so it will be easier to transport. Be sure to bring it back home at the end of the day."

Her mom was always baking something for one function or another, not to mention just to have something on hand if friends stopped by for tea, someone died, or if someone was in need. As busy as owning Mariner's Fish Fry restaurant kept her mother, Katelyn didn't know when she had time to bake. Dawn Sullivan spent more time in the kitchen than bakers at the local bakery, especially during the Thanksgiving and Christmas holiday season. Katelyn sighed as her mother took her reindeer apron off and hung it over the chair.

"I'm going to the restaurant early this morning and start baking for the Sunday crowd."

If she didn't hold back eating her mother's baked goods and watch her calorie intake, she was going to have to enroll in an exercise program in order to keep the pounds off. She needed to keep in shape for when Sven finally agreed on a wedding date. She wanted to look spectacular in her wedding gown—the one she hadn't bought yet. She'd drooled over the lovely display Kelly Andrews always had in the window at Wedded Bliss every time she passed by. One day soon she was going to stop in and try on gowns, maybe even have Kelly plan her wedding.

Katelyn had always enjoyed participating in community projects when she was a teenager, especially if they involved children. Part of the high school's community credit curriculum was to volunteer at a local food pantry, children's programs, or various other outreach programs. This year, her father had roped her into working at his lodge's annual Breakfast with Santa event—a special event where children got to enjoy a free breakfast with Santa. Her mother was right—she enjoyed watching the young and young-at-heart sit on Santa's lap while they told him what they wanted for Christmas. It gave her pleasure to watch their eyes open in awe and sparkle with merriment. Santa had gifts for everyone brave enough to sit on his lap. She remembered the first time her parents had taken her to Breakfast with Santa. She was three and she had screamed bloody murder the entire time. She wouldn't sit on his lap, didn't dare get near him, and cried when she left because she wanted to go back and give him a hug. The only thing different today? She wasn't going to be the one screaming when she locked eyes on Santa—whoever he was. It would be part of her job to help calm the panicked children when they spotted him and cried. She commiserated with them. Santa was bigger than life and a bit intimidating. Her own experiences at that age had been scary, to say the least.

Thankfully she wouldn't be the only elf there. Blanca and Cara Cruz, twins who both were attending U.C. Berkeley, were home for winter break, and had also been volunteered to help. But unlike her, they were excited to don their outfits and spice up their act.

An inch of snow had fallen during the night—it sparkled magically in the bright morning sun that was in the process of lifting the fog from the ground. Not a breeze stirred, not a cloud scarred the clear blue sky over Frenchman Bay. In fact, it was almost sweater weather—unusual for a Lobster Cove winter, along Maine's eastern coast. Katelyn threw a red lamb's wool cape around her shoulders. She smiled despite herself as she realized it matched her outfit perfectly. She scuffed out of her pointy slippers and slipped into a pair of black furry ankle-high boots, and then drew the cape hood over her head for the walk to the lodge.

"I'm leaving now," she called to her mother.

"Have a good time, dear. Don't forget to take the pies."

"Got 'em. Bye." She caught one last look in the hall mirror before she went out the door. Now she looked like Little Red Riding Hood with a basket of goodies.

Katelyn walked the two blocks to the lodge. At seven a.m. the sidewalks had already been cleared of snow. She kept her eyes straight ahead hoping no one would recognize her in her get-up. As much as she was glad Sven wouldn't see her in this god-awful outfit, she was disappointed he was missing one of Lobster Cove's annual events for children of all ages. Which made her think of her best friend, Juelle McClintock, who was now married and living in Oahu, Hawaii, for the winter. She missed their talks, and especially Juelle's daughter Makenzie who she had babysat for many times during Juelle's first husband's accident and subsequent death. After finding out he'd been having an affair, her friend deserved to find love again, even if it was in the form of another McClintock—the real heir to the McClintock and McClintock Lobster business. Only this time the McClintock and McClintock stood for Hunter and Juelle McClintock. She chuckled. Juelle so deserved love and happiness. Juelle's ex-mother-in-law Eugenia hadn't made her life easy. But that was all in the past.

Katelyn stopped at the intersection to check for traffic. A car pulled up, honked at her. She looked up to see one of the Scout leaders wave, give her a big smile, and a thumbs up. He waited for her to cross before he continued. She waved as she crossed the street. So much for not being recognized. She dragged her feet as she made her way up the front steps to the lodge. She took a moment to put a smile on her face to prepare to go inside and play elf. Before she turned the doorknob, the door opened to the small, but imposing lodge.

"Hi, Katelyn. Glad you could make it." Carl Claussen stood inside to welcome everyone. "Miss Red, I presume. Don't you look fun?"

"Thanks, Mr. Claussen. Looking forward to working with the children." No lie. She was actually looking forward to interacting with all the little ones, despite her angst over the costume. She loved kids, and had chosen to major in child development, and was finishing her master's degree and her teaching certificate. The only dark cloud hanging over her shoulders was the loss of her own child years ago. Still able to have children, she hoped someday soon she and Sven would have a little girl or boy of their own to love. But first, she had to tie Sven down to a wedding date—he'd been dragging his feet the past year.

"Here, let me take those pies for you," Carl said,

holding his hands out for them. "I'll see Maude gets them. Why don't you join the other elves so you can plan your strategy? Cara and Blanca are already suited up and in the kitchen. The Boy Scouts will be here soon to cover clearing tables and dishwashing duties. Santa will be coming down the stairs any minute."

Katelyn ducked through the side door into the kitchen. Cara and Blanca, a few years younger, were in the midst of pointing fingers at each other and laughing at their ridiculous outfits. In truth, she looked a smidge better than they did, which wasn't saying much.

"Katelyn," the two chorused at the same time.

"Hi. How are things going at Berkeley, ladies?"

"Awesome."

"Great. Do you feel as stupid as we do in these getups?" Blanca asked, clearly enjoying the whole experience.

Blanca's smile, however, was contagious. Their bubbly company lifted Katelyn's spirits. She smiled at the two elves, even though butterflies were doing a wicked dance inside her stomach at having to wear this getup in a room full of people she knew.

"Worse than stupid. But, hey, it's for the kids, right? I'm sure we won't look stupid to them." Katelyn's mother's words slipped out of her mouth, which gave them meaning, and an attitude adjustment that she so badly needed. "Do you know who's playing Santa this year?"

"No." Cara glanced at Blanca, silently asking her sister.

"No idea," Blanca responded. "But I hear it's some new guy in town who recently joined the lodge. Or the Boy Scout Troop. Mr. Claussen didn't say for sure."

"Probably a good thing, seeing as we might spill the beans to one of the kids," Cara said.

"Ho, ho, ho, ho, ho," a deep voice rang out from the hallway. "Merry Christmas. Ho, ho, ho." Bells jingled at his approach, drawing everyone's attention.

Katelyn joined the two girls in the main dining room as Santa took his seat in the far corner next to the pine-scented Christmas tree covered in multi-colored blinking lights, the star on top a bit lopsided. The only visible feature of the tall, somewhat hefty man was Santa's eyes, and even they were hidden behind a pair of glasses with hazy lenses. And from a distance, there was no way to tell their color. Outfitted in the traditional red and white suit, beard, hat, and a pair of black boots, not an inch of skin or hair was left uncovered. The man was big, or else he was sufficiently padded. From where she stood across the room, his right hand held a set of gold jingle bells, and his left was hooked in his wide black belt. He looked like the real deal. The kids were sure to enjoy sitting on his lap. She hoped whoever it was liked kids and had a great sense of humor.

As soon as the first family arrived with two small boys between the ages of three and five, Santa proceeded to shake his fist full of bells, again—the musical tone filled the big hall, and immediately drew their attention. They ran to Santa, stopped just short of jumping onto his lap, and stood stock still, staring in awe. Santa leaned over to talk to them, and then lifted them both on to his lap, on opposite knees. The room began to fill, and Katelyn, Blanca, and Cara began working the room, making sure everyone had a chance to visit with the big guy in the red suit.

Things slowed down two hours later. The aroma of pancakes, eggs, and sausage had Katelyn's stomach crying out for food. Cara and Blanca had taken a break earlier, and she waved to them, indicating she was about to escape. She made her way past the Boy Scouts snapping towels and splashing water from their fingers at each other. Two elderly lodge members wearing red Santa caps with large white pompoms, filled plates to those lined up on the other side of the counter. She smiled at them, grabbed a plate, filled it with pancakes, covered them with fresh, homemade maple syrup, and made her way to the kitchen. Keeping out of the way of the men flipping pancakes and scrambling eggs at the old-fashioned black gas stove, she found a seat at the far end of an empty table. She set her plate on the table, pulled up a chair, and quickly ate her pancakes so she could get back to helping Blanca and Cara assist Santa. A Santa who kept staring at her as if he recognized her. Or couldn't get past the horrible image she presented in her pathetic outfit. She stood, pulled at the hem of her miniskirt, and then carted her plate out to the Scouts to be cleaned. She washed the sticky syrup off her hands, applied a fresh coat of lipstick, took a deep breath, plopped her cap back on her head, and pasted a smile on her face. The dining hall was bursting at the seams with holiday cheer and kids hyped up on Santa and syrup when she walked back in.

"Katelyn, don't you look cute dressed as an elf. What a great idea."

Katelyn groaned as one of the Scout leaders cornered her on her way past the Scouts. Two of the Boy Scouts stopped fooling around and looked her way. Really looked at her for the first time, and grinned.

"Looking hot," one of the older Scouts said before they both turned back to washing dishes.

Crap! More attention than she wanted.

Katelyn dashed past them only to have Santa look her way when she walked in. He was doing it again. Nodding and smiling. And unnerving her. She was going to have words with her father after today's event ended. At twenty-six, she was just too old to be parading around as an elf. The darn outfit was drawing too much attention. She tugged at her miniskirt. Good Lord, he was watching her again. Was the man a pervert?

"Watch out, Katelyn," Cara shouted, stepping in front of her, leaning forward to rescue yet another frantic frightened child running away from Santa, screaming and heading hell-bent-for-election right at Katelyn's knees.

Gads! It was going to be a long morning.

****

Mark had all he could do to keep his eyes and mind on the kids all morning. Carrying on a conversation while watching Katelyn Sullivan out of the corner of his eyes was driving him nuts. She was more beautiful now than she had been six years ago. And hot damn, the elf outfit was just about the sexiest getup he'd seen in a long time. On her, it was like a beacon sending out come-hither signals, like the lighthouse next to her parent's restaurant. And he had no trouble receiving those signals—loud and clear. They had drifted apart after high school when she went off to attend college and he joined the military. Was she in a relationship now? There'd been rumors, but folks in town weren't being very forthcoming with details. Lobster Cove's rumor mill tended to be part myth, part truth, and all wrong sometimes, if he remembered correctly. Hell, he could only imagine what they'd been spreading about him—where he had disappeared to, and why he was back with a two-year-old son in tow. Secret missions for the military left little room for confiding in family or sharing secrets with loved ones. Not sure what his parents had told anyone, but he did know they'd kept his career and his wife's death to themselves. Of course, they didn't know the entire story, either.

Dammit! He was tired of guarding secrets.

Katelyn herded a pair of twin boys in his direction. His heart raced as she drew near enough for him to touch her. Instead, he lifted the two four-year-olds on to his knees.

"Ho, ho, ho, Miss Elf. Who do we have here?" He looked directly into her eyes instead of the boys', hoping she'd recognize him.

She didn't.

"This is Ryan and Ethan Holmes, Santa. They have a list for you to take back to the North Pole."

Mark ignored the list and continued gazing into Katelyn's baby blues. The boys wiggled, diverting his attention back to the main reason he was there—to play Santa. He sighed as she walked away, and vowed he'd find an opportunity to talk to her before the end of the day.

It seemed ages before there was a break in the action. Everyone was busy eating or playing with the toys he'd handed out. The damn beard was getting itchy and his neck was sweating up a storm—rivulets of sweat trickled down his back. And if he wasn't mistaken, the front of his pants was a bit wet where one of the babies had sat with a soggy diaper. He didn't really mind, he was used to dealing with his own little boy from the time Kurtis was a baby. He hoped his son wouldn't catch on that he was playing Santa when his parents arrived with him in tow. Others hadn't figured it out yet, but then he hadn't been in town for the last six years, so not many of the younger kids would know him. His heart swelled just thinking about how precious his own son had become over the past two years. Being a parent was priority one. He had to keep that in mind. The reason he was back in Lobster Cove.

While the children were occupied with their breakfast, Mark stood, stretched, and then started working the room. He leaned over and whispered in ears, gave out hugs, and made it a point to engage those who hadn't dare sit on his lap. When he reached the back of the room where the three adult elves were gathered, he determined now was his chance to speak to Katelyn. See if she remembered him.

"So, my little Elves, are you ready to sit on Santa's lap and tell me what good little girls you've been all year?"

"Oh, Santa," one of the elves crooned. "I thought you'd never ask."

Oh, my, God! Was that little Cara Cruz? With a pierced nose?

"It's much too crowded in here with all these children running around, I don't think it would look at all proper for one of your elves to sit on your lap in front of them. Perhaps later when we're alone?" The other one purred, and gave him a wink.

Mark gulped. Oh, my, God! Cara's twin, Blanca? Her short hair made her look like a sexy business woman now, a grown-up version of her bad-girl twin. As elves, they looked more like double trouble personified. Didn't need to go there.

He leaned toward Katelyn, slipped an arm around her shoulders, and drew her in for a hug.

"Ho, ho, ho, Miss Elf. And what do you want for Christmas?"

The contact was electrifying clear down to his black fur-lined hotter-than-hell boots. He wiggled his toes and had a hard time controlling his voice. He had to let go of her or embarrass himself right then and there—fat red suit or no fat red suit, Santa had to keep up appearances in a room full of kids. But, God forgive him, he didn't want to let her go. He hadn't wanted to let her go six years ago, but he'd had no choice back then. He didn't want to drag her into the kind of military life he'd signed up for. Now? Hell if he knew what he was doing—dredging up the past.

Katelyn frowned, shook her head, and stepped away. His arm dropped to his side. He latched on to his thick black belt and pretended to shake his belly, and focused on the twins. "Ho, ho, ho. I think I better double-check my list. Sounds like you two might have been naughtier than you're letting on."

The two girls giggled like ten-year-olds, their hands flew to their ample chests, and damned if they didn't both just wink at him again. Katelyn, on the other hand, simply shook her head and turned her back on them.

"I think you'd better get back to your post, Santa. There's a new line of anxious children waiting."

Damn. She was right. And it looked as if they were about to help themselves to the sack of goodies and the dish of candy canes he'd left sitting next to his chair, unattended. He raised his left hand and gave the jingle bells a hearty shake. "Ho, ho, ho," he called on his way to the front of the room.

Two of the young girls in line began to cry. Their mother scooped one of them up, and the poor distraught child wrapped her arms around her mother's neck and clung for dear life. One of the smaller boys shoved another into the tree. The branches swayed and two of the bulbs hit the floor. Thankfully, they were unbreakable.

Before he walked to his throne-type chair, Katelyn and the other elves were on the scene putting order to the chaos. Candy canes were handed out to those waiting their turn.

Someone plugged in a CD player, and Christmas tunes blared into the room. Half the parents in the middle of eating pancakes erupted into song with none other than "Santa Claus is Coming to Town." The rest of them joined in. The young ones clapped their hands, and a few even started dancing around the tables. He should have been pleased with the turn of events— everyone was having a ball.

Mark had been away for so long he'd forgotten how Lobster Cove's close-knit community treated everyone like family. He hadn't expected to be thrown back into the thick of things quite so soon. He hadn't expected Katelyn to give him the cold shoulder so effectively. But then, he really hadn't expected her to greet him with open arms. Damn. His life was half a mess—he was still picking up the pieces after his wife's untimely death, dealing with a child, and looking to start over in the States.

Dear, God. How am I ever going to handle coming home this Christmas after seeing Katie dressed like a sexy elf?

Chapter Two

Katelyn took off her winter outerwear, kicked off her boots and slipped into her sneakers. She loved working at the Hearts and Hands Daycare as part of her class project for credit. She joined Linda Claussen, Carl's wife, and Carolyn Clark, one of the part-time daycare providers, in the small kitchen area where they were preparing morning snacks for the children.

"So, have you heard Mark Logan is back in town?" Linda asked.

Katelyn didn't reply. She was more than aware of who Mark Logan was—Linda didn't have to mention his last name. She hadn't seen him yet, but her mother told her he was back in Lobster Cove. He hadn't contacted her since high school. In fact, it was as if he didn't exist. Not even his parents had mentioned him in all those years—to anyone. And in a small community like Lobster Cove, it was unusual. The rumor mill had been silent in regards to Mark Logan.

Until now.

For all she knew, he was married with a family.

Parents started to arrive with their children, ending their conversation, and giving Katelyn a reprieve from replying to Linda's question. The day progressed and Katelyn was lost in a world of joy as she played with the children, read to them, helped them with their craft projects, and then helped them put on their winter garments at the end of the day. She waved goodbye to the last parent and kid for the day—Connie Blye, a single mother who was late picking up her son, Jason. Again. But Katelyn didn't mind. Single parents had it tough holding down a job, trying to make ends meet, and raising a child on their own. After all, if she hadn't miscarried in her second month, it could be her.

Many of the children in Hearts and Hands Daycare, like Jason, were the products of broken homes, or single mothers left high and dry to fend the best they could after their husbands had met their fates on the open seas, or in the military. Thankfully, the majority of these parents had support from their own parents, and the community. Thanks to Eugenia McClintock's annual donation to several organizations like the Hearts and Hands Daycare, the funding helped provide an excellent program for the children, keeping the cost to attend low for the parents.

"Late again, huh?" Linda called from behind the small kitchenette enclosure, the overhead flap swinging shut for the night. She and Linda hadn't had a chance to talk, other than to discuss the events for the day's agenda.

"Yes, but I don't mind. She wasn't that late coming home from work. Besides, Jason is such a doll. No trouble at all. He loves spending time on his own in the reading corner or playing with the building blocks."

"You're too accommodating."

"We have to be here to close for the night, anyway. You know I love these little kids, so it's no problem."

"Did you hear me this morning? Did you know Mark Logan was back in town?"

"Yes, the rumor mill is alive and well." She

chastised herself for being disappointed she hadn't run into him yet. After all, he was in the past. Sven was her future.

"I know you had a thing for him back in high school."

Little did Linda know about her "thing" for Mark. No one knew about her pregnancy, and she wanted to keep it that way.

"That was a long time ago. We haven't kept in touch since graduation. I'm sure he's moved on with his life. He's probably forgotten all about me." Katelyn set the tray of plastic cups, now half empty of various colors of washable paint and matching brushes, on the counter.

"Yes. I hear he joined the military—became a big deal. One of those Navy SEALs. Secret Service. Or Special Ops Commandos. Or something no one can talk about. His parents have been very hush-hush about what he's been doing all these years—where he's been."

Katelyn hadn't seen Mark's parents around town much—they kept to themselves after Mark graduated and joined the military. She had spent a lot of time at the Logans' home when she and Mark had dated. They'd always been kind. They'd been like second parents. But when she and Mark broke it off and they'd each gone their separate ways, her path never crossed with the Logans. She'd seen them a few times at St. Joseph's Church, but they mostly kept to themselves.

Linda finished washing a handful of dishes and stacked them in the drain board, and then wiped her hands on a paper towel.

"The sink is all yours."

"Thanks." Katelyn rinsed the leftover non-toxic paint in the sink, and ran the brushes under the spray from the faucet. The colors blended, swirling together in a kaleidoscopic fashion before gurgling down the drain. She placed the cups and brushes in the sudsy water to wash.

"Hey, I forgot to ask, how did playing elf go at the lodge on Sunday?" Linda picked up a towel to dry the dishes in the drying rack.

"Don't ask. We had to wear skimpy elf outfits. I looked more like a circus clown than an elf. My father convinced the lodge members it would be 'the cat's pajamas' to have elves there this year. I told him I was too old to be playing an elf, but I was speaking to deaf ears. Didn't Carl fill you in?"

Linda laughed—despite her age, and having grown children of her own, she was always ready for anything—the zanier the better, and her husband, Carl, had a great sense of humor, as well—the two made a great couple. She was a fun coworker—the kids loved her.

"I bet the kids had a ball, didn't they? Who filled in for Mr. Unger this year? Carl didn't say. After Mr. Unger had his heart attack in January, he and his wife packed it in and went to Florida. Carl said they both love it down there."

Mr. Unger was one of the older members of the lodge and a real sweetie. He'd always done a superb job playing Santa, his naturally white hair helped fool the kids. And the kids adored him.

"Dad didn't say, either." Katelyn shook her head. "He just handed me the elf outfit and told me I'd look great all decked out. Whoever it was, the kids loved him."

"Carl said Santa was already upstairs putting on his outfit when he arrived."

She was glad whoever played Santa this year had put his heart and soul into it. Katelyn froze in the process of wringing out a cloth. Whoever it was probably considered her a dork in that god-awful outfit the way he'd kept looking at her and smiling. Or, was it leering?

She proceeded to sponge the paint spatter off the plastic smocks the kids wore when they painted, and then dried them with a paper towel.

"Any kids from the daycare attend?"

"Most of them. Where were you, by the way?"

"Had to finish a few projects at home. Was Mark there with his little boy?"

Katelyn swung around to face Linda. "Excuse me? Mark has a little boy?" She shouldn't be surprised. After all, she'd figured he'd moved on after graduation. However, in his line of work, she assumed he hadn't time for a family—he hadn't had time for her. The rumor mill was slipping—it hadn't mentioned Mark had a child. How had they kept that a secret?

That meant he had a wife, and they were all here in Lobster Cove.

"Oops. I see you didn't know. Sorry. I can't believe he didn't take his son to Breakfast with Santa. Jan said he might enroll him at Hearts and Hands. But it hasn't been confirmed yet."

"He wasn't there—at least I didn't see him. I didn't know Mark was married or that he had a son."

Oh my God! Mark had a son! Tears welled in her eyes. She looked away so Linda wouldn't see how hard this piece of news had hit her. She'd lost a son—his son! And he had a son—with another woman. The irony was staggering.

"My impression was the military was his whole life."

"Guess he met someone he couldn't live without. Oh, drat. Sorry, Katelyn, didn't mean it the way it sounded."

"It was a long time ago. Like I said, we both went our separate ways right after high school."

Why hadn't she seen Mark and his son at Breakfast with Santa? Had they arrived when she was in the kitchen eating? How old was his son? How could he have fallen in love with someone else so soon after high school? After confessing his love for her? The idea of him with a son brought her to her knees. She had to get out of there, away from Linda, before the flood gates opened and she made a spectacle of herself.

"Carl's ordering our special—pizza, and a movie on the tube tonight. Want to join us? The girls will be home for a change. It won't be like you're a third wheel or anything."

"Thanks, but no. In fact, if you don't mind, I need to get going. I need to get to Mariner's to help the folks with the dinner crowd tonight. Mom's got one of her specials going. It's sure to be packed."

"You go ahead. I'll finish here."

"Are you sure you don't mind?"

"Carl has everything for tonight under control. Go. I'm almost ready to close anyway. I'll practically follow you out the door."

She knew Linda didn't mean to hurt her feelings. She was unaware of hers and Mark's split six years ago—didn't know about her miscarriage. Linda had hit a sore spot that obviously hadn't healed. Implying she wasn't the "one" for Mark was nothing short of depressing. And it didn't help to learn he'd married and had a little boy. And they had returned home, and were living in Lobster Cove.

It should have been her little boy. Hers and Mark's.

****

The rest of the week flew by. Katelyn put the finishing touches on her final reports for the end of semester classes, and then put in as much time at the Hearts and Hands Daycare as she could fit in. She needed to keep busy—keep her mind off Mark and his son. Friday night found her filling in at her parent's restaurant again. Mariner's was hopping after the high school basketball game. Several groups of students were hanging out in their usual booths in the far end of the dining area, keeping Katelyn busy busing burgers and fries and lobster rolls—the smell of hot beef on the grill and lobster boiling permeated the air.

Families with small children filled the center tables, while couples occupied the tables closer to the window overlooking the bay. Dawn Sullivan kept the groups of families happy, and Katelyn concentrated on waiting on the teens. By the time she had delivered their platters, it felt as if she had already run a marathon and served a million burgers and lobster rolls. Unfortunately, it hadn't done a thing to take her mind off the news that Mark Logan was back in town, or that Sven was in Norway. Sven hadn't contacted her since he'd called to tell her he'd arrived in Bergen.

She wasn't sure how she should feel about Mark

coming home. It had been a long time—they had each gone their separate ways. But memories surfaced and tugged at her chest all evening, reviving feelings she'd thought were buried forever. What would she say when she did see him? And with his wife and son by his side? What would she do? She was curious to find out what he'd been doing all these years, but then again, she wasn't sure she really wanted to know.

He had been tall, dark, and drop-dead gorgeous in high school. One of the star football players. Would he be more handsome, and powerfully built after his life-style in the military? Would she recognize him?

Would he recognize her?

Why was she letting it get to her? She was engaged to Sven now. She had to let it go or she'd make herself crazy.

She was relieved when the last customer left for the evening. She joined her mother in the alcove next to the kitchen entrance, ready to kick off her shoes.

"I'm beat."

"We've had a successful evening despite the snowflakes outside."

"It's Lobster Cove, Mom, everyone is used to a few snowflakes. At least it's not a wet snow, and the roads aren't slippery. Do you need me to help cash out tonight? You're looking tired. Why don't you call it a night and I'll finish here?"

"No, no. I have to wait for your father, anyway. You go on home and put your feet up. You look tired—a little pale. Are you okay? You've been working day and night the last few weeks. When are your classes over?"

"My last exam is Monday. I'll have plenty of time

to study over the weekend."

"Have you heard from Sven? He's been gone a whole week now. You must miss him. When is he supposed to come home?"

Katelyn had no answers. She'd wondered the same thing. Would he be home in time for Christmas?

"I don't know. I hope soon."

"Have you seen Mark yet? I know this must be hard for you, honey, but you're going to have to face him sooner or later."

"There is nothing to gain by 'facing' him. I understand he's married and has a son." She couldn't hide her shaky voice. Tears threatened, but she held them back.

"Oh, my dear. I'm so sorry." Her mother pulled her in for a hug. She let her. "You know we're here for you. Anything you need."

Katelyn hugged her mother, wanting to cry on her shoulder. But she wasn't eighteen any longer. She was more mature than that—or at least considered herself mature. "Thanks. You and Dad have been a rock. I love you both. I think I will go home and call it a night if you don't mind."

"Not at all. Like I said, I have to wait for your father."

Katelyn rushed to the employee's locker room and put on her blue woolen coat, hat, and gloves. Her shoes were sturdy enough to weather what little snow had fallen. She stepped outside, welcoming the clear, cold, frosty air nipping her nose, which brought her back to the present. The snow had stopped, so there was no need to brush off the windshield. Her ride home was a short one through the now deserted streets. Green garlands hung draped across Main Street adorned with large red bows in the center. Wreaths decorated the lamp posts, and every store front twinkled and shone brightly and reflected onto the empty roadway. The loneliness of the night resonated deep inside, despite the colorful streets.

****

Saturday morning turned out to be another crisp, clear day in Lobster Cove. A perfect day to take Kurtis to pick out a Christmas tree at the lodge where the Boy Scouts were set up for the day. Mark walked the shoveled path, circling the cut Christmas trees. A few trees leaned against the building, others were tied to a rope like clothes on a clothes line on the other side of the path. Kurtis' arms were wound tight around his neck as he squirmed to get a better look at the trees. He was pleased to see his son's cheeks a rosy shade, even if it was from the cool morning breeze off the harbor— a color that had been missing for some time. Mark had given up so much in order to bring him home to be around family. He knew Kurtis missed having a mother. The kid needed more than a passel of babysitters. He needed stability. Would he find it here in Lobster Cove? He couldn't think of a better place to start, than with his parents.

Katie came to mind—seeing her last Sunday at Breakfast with Santa had warm memories of their time together in high school flooding his mind. He understood she was in her last year of university, and engaged to be married. His mother had mentioned it in passing. He hadn't expected Katie to wait for him— they had parted on friendly terms, each going their separate ways. But he hadn't expected her to attend

Breakfast with Santa, and certainly not looking hotter-than-hell in that elf getup. She had filled out in all the right places since he'd seen her last. She was one sexy lady. His heart had just about jumped out of his chest the minute he spotted her. Just his luck she was about to be taken off the eligible list. Talk about bad timing.

Mark circled around another row of mid-sized evergreen trees, their branches spread out with a bit of snow clinging to a few of the lower branches.

"That one." Kurtis pointed, his red mitten making it difficult to see which tree he wanted.

"Let's look around a bit more, bud. We need the right one to take home to Grandma."

"Grandma?"

"Yep. You've got a grandma and a grandpa now. We'll be there for Christmas."

"You, too?"

"Yep. I'm not going anywhere. We'll be together, always."

Kurtis planted a cold, wet kiss on Mark's cheek. An emotional tear formed, but he smiled, continued, and then stopped in front of another tree. He was always amazed at the emotional tug his son had on his heart. Kurtis jumped up and down in his arms like a monkey, excited when he spotted a black dog with a red collar and bow around its neck sitting in front of the tree.

"Dog."

"Yes, it's a black lab puppy."

"Want puppy."

"Not sure Grandma and Grandpa Logan are ready for a puppy, bud. They have us to deal with—for now."

Maybe when they'd settled in, found a place of

their own, he'd consider getting Kurtis a puppy.

"Want puppy." Kurtis' plea grew louder. He held Mark's cheeks in his mitten-covered hands, and stared into his eyes. It was hard to say no.

"Maybe someday we can have a puppy. But not now. Now, we need to pick out a tree so we can take it home and decorate it."

"Tree. I want that one."

Finally.

"Yep. That one will do. Let's go tell one of the Boy Scouts to load it on the roof of the car so we can take it home."

Home. God that had a lovely ring to it. He and Natasha hadn't even had a chance to buy a home. They'd lived in a small, unobtrusive apartment boasting one extra room he'd made into a nursery for Kurtis. For the most part, his life in the military had been a solitary one. Natasha had been on the Russian team with him, and for the first year they had worked together. Their relationship had been totally platonic—but that had changed over time. They certainly hadn't expected to become parents. They married—it had been the right thing to do. After she gave birth to Kurtis, Natasha had gone back to working Special Ops. She'd been sent on assignment without him. The team had been ambushed and she'd been fatally shot. The entire operation had been in question from the get-go, but she'd insisted on taking part.

He mourned her loss, of course, but he'd had Kurtis to raise. And raising a son on his own wasn't easy. Still wasn't, but trying to remain undercover and retain a modicum of secrecy was neither beneficial to him, nor Kurtis—not to mention damn difficult. It was time to call it quits when he'd learned of a kidnapping plot against his son. His directors weren't happy when he'd told them he wanted out. In fact, they were irate, and tried to talk him out of leaving the force. They offered him plenty of incentives to stay, but he adamantly refused—at first. However, when they offered him a position with the Department of Homeland Security stateside, letting him choose Maine as his home base, he couldn't resist. And honestly, standing here, right now, with Kurtis wrapped around his neck, gawking at the string of lights glittering around the fenced-in area, with dozens of Christmas trees, and seeing the wonder shining in his son's big blue eyes, it was worth foregoing a promotion and settling back home any day of the week.

Mark circled the last row of trees and headed for the stand to ask one of the Scouts to bundle the tree for him, and stopped in his tracks. Kurtis tightened his hold on Mark's neck. Mark's throat closed, and it wasn't from Kurtis pressing against his Adam's apple. Katelyn Sullivan stood next to the check-out stand talking to the two Scouts on the other side of the make-shift wooden structure. Whatever they were talking about, it made her laugh. Memories stirred. The sound was music to his ears. And it didn't help that she looked sexier than she had in her elf outfit. Those tight blue jeans, tall black leather boots, a blue quilted jacket with matching scarf, and a winter cap covering her beautiful blonde hair, with a few wisps sticking out, had his heart stuck in his throat. She should be on the cover of a L.L. Bean catalogue. He took a deep breath, and then, taking his chances, stepped closer, shifting Kurtis to his other arm.

She turned. And froze. Her eyes wide with what he

could only assume were shock. After all, he'd already seen her, and he was certain she hadn't recognized him in his Santa outfit.

"Mark?"

"It's been a long time, Katie. How are you?"

She stared at Kurtis, then back at him. She looked stunned.

She looked amazing.

She smelled of apple blossom shampoo—he knew because that's what she always used—it reminded him of crisp autumn days, football games, and Katie on the sidelines, cheering.

"This is Kurtis. My son. Kurtis, say hi to my friend, Katie."

"Hi, Katie. I'm Kurtis."

"Um…ah…hi, Kurtis. It's nice to meet you. Have you found a tree yet?"

"We were just about to have one of the Scouts load it up on the car for us. What about you? Are you here to pick out a tree? Are you alone?" He was digging for information, something he usually excelled at covertly, but even this was a bit obvious. He looked around to see if she was alone, or if there was someone with her—a man? Her fiancé?

"Yes, I'm here to pick out my tree. Sven, my fiancé, is in Norway with his parents visiting his grandparents for the next couple of weeks. But I was anxious to get started on my decorations. Christmas is my favorite time of year."

"Yes, I remember." Damn. She *was* engaged. His mother was right. Still, having her confirm it had a lump the size of a mortar round hit his gut with a thud.

"What about you? Visiting your parents?"

"Actually, I'm staying with them—for now. They've been kind enough to take us in until we can find a house and get settled."

"Oh? You're moving back to Lobster Cove?"

"That's my plan. What about you? You and your fiancé plan on staying in Lobster Cove?" He wanted to tell her how great she looked. Wanted to keep her talking—anything to keep her standing there even though he was making himself miserable wishing things between them had been different. Wishing they hadn't drifted apart. 'Cause his libido was going crazy standing this close to her. Would he be overstepping the fiancé thing if he took her in his arms and gave her a hug? He stepped closer, remembered he had Kurtis in his arms, and then shifted him to his other arm, again. Damn, she'd stepped to the side, her facial expression pale despite the cold breeze blowing around the now crowded tree stand.

"Mister? You want to show me the tree you picked out? I'll load it for you."

"Yeah. Sure. It's back here."

"Tree." Kurtis put a cold mitten on Mark's face, and twisted his face around to meet his. Between the Scout and his son distracting him, Katelyn had started to walk down a different path—away from him.

"I'll see you around," he called. "Maybe we can get together for coffee…or dinner at Mariners?"

She waved and called goodbye, and was out of sight among the trees before he could breathe again. Based on her reaction, having dinner with Katelyn Sullivan didn't look promising. He needed to get on with his life—let the past go and concentrate on his son.

Easier said than done. After seeing her again, it

was going to be impossible.

"Mister? You need help with that tree, or what?"

Chapter Three

Katelyn couldn't get away from Mark fast enough. He'd called her Katie in that deep, sexy tone of voice that had always driven her insides wild. No one called her Katie, least of all Sven. It was always Katelyn. Gads, his look had shot straight to her heart and made her long to be held in his arms once again—those strong, enticing arms that had always been comforting, loving. She wanted nothing more, at that moment, than to have his arms encircle her, pull her close, recapture those long ago emotions they'd shared. Comfort her. She wanted to confide in him. Tell him about their pregnancy—their miscarriage. How she'd tried to get the nerve to reach out to him, try to locate him, but too emotionally depleted after losing their child, she hadn't been able to find the courage or the strength. She'd turned inside herself for so long, her parents urging her out of her shell. They had been so supportive in her decision to go on to college as planned. And with her choice of career—working with children even though it would never erase what she had lost—it would help fill the void in her heart.

She sighed as she walked along the narrow path between the sweet smelling scents of fresh snow, evergreens, and the salty ocean blowing off the bay. What an idiot she'd been—standing there tongue-tied, lusting after an old boyfriend when she was engaged to

Sven. And Mark had married and had a son. Where was his wife? No one had mentioned her, including Mark. Linda had warned her he had a child, but it hadn't actually affected her as much as it did seeing them in person, just now. Together.

It was obvious Mark enjoyed fatherhood—loved his son—they looked so right together. Happy. Kurtis looked like his father—the same Icelandic blue eyes, dark, wavy hair, and that sexy dimple in his left cheek when he smiled.

A lump formed in her throat. She shook her head and straightened her shoulders—and stomped around the end of the first row of trees. The excitement of searching for the right tree sank clear to the bottom of her leather boots. Emotionally drained, she was ready to turn around and go home.

Her fiancé was absent, her ex-boyfriend was married and had a son, and her best friend, Juelle, had remarried and was now living in Hawaii. She, on the other hand, had no one to help celebrate Christmas. Still reeling from having had to dress as an elf and embarrassing herself in front of the entire town of Lobster Cove, she was ready to pack it in and call it quits. Even another cup of hot cocoa with marshmallows in front of a roaring fire in an empty room wasn't going to do the trick when she got home. And right now, any tree would do.

"Rudolph the Red Nosed Reindeer" blared over the loudspeaker, bells jingled. Cars brimming with anxious children excited to get out and pick out their trees, pulled in. She grabbed the first tree, a few inches taller than her, one she could handle when she got home. She hailed the nearest Scout for help, and then followed him, the tree thrown over his sturdy shoulder, back to the stand.

After she paid for the tree, the Scout loaded it onto the top of her car, securing it with elastic ties for the short ride home. She pulled into her drive, ignored the tree on top of the vehicle looking like a sadly neglected tree from Whoville, and went inside. She started the CD player—Christmas music automatically kicked in. She was in dire need of something to help lift her spirits, but music alone wasn't going to do it.

She started a fire in the fireplace, and then stood and surveyed the room empty of decorations. It looked cold and lonely despite the fire that was starting to crackle in the grate. What she needed was the tree set up so she could decorate it, and whip the place into something more festive—at least it would be a start. It was time to pull the tree off the car, and drag it inside before she settled in with a cup of hot cocoa.

Strains of "Blue Christmas" followed her to the front door. She missed Sven. But her mind shifted to Mark Logan. It had been a shock to see him. Her emotions always high during the holidays, seeing Mark with his son, didn't help.

Katelyn trudged to the door. Prepared to drag the tree inside, she swung the door wide, and gasped. She hadn't expected to come face to face with Mark and Kurtis standing on her front porch so soon.

"Hi, again." His smile had her insides fluttering as if a swarm of baby butterflies were fighting it out inside.

"Hi. Is something wrong?" Her mind shut down.

"No. Kurtis was concerned you didn't have someone to help you with your tree. He suggested we give you a hand. I see it's still on the car."

Speechless. Thrilled. Turned on by his sexy good looks, she didn't know what to say. It wasn't a good idea to let him help her. In fact, it was a bad idea to let him inside. She looked around him, expecting to see his wife sitting in the car.

Nope. No one.

As if he read her mind, he said, "It's just me and Kurtis. Natasha is no longer with us."

"Natasha is your wife?"

"Was my wife. Long story, short—she died shortly after Kurtis was born."

"Oh, Mark, I'm sorry to hear of your loss." How devastating. Poor Kurtis. She looked down at his questioning expression. Did he miss not having a mother?

"So, Kurtis suggested it, did he?" She smiled at the small boy who hadn't taken his eyes off her all the while he hung on to his father's hand, his head resting against Mark's leg.

"Tree." Kurtis pointed to the car.

"Perfect timing. I was just about to drag it inside. Guess I could use some help, after all."

"If it's okay, Kurtis can wait on the porch."

"He can wait inside where it's warm."

"Cocoa. Want hot cocoa."

"Kurtis! That's not polite. We'll have hot cocoa when we get back to grandma's house."

"Want cocoa, now."

"No—"

"Of course he can have some hot cocoa. I was about to have a cup myself." She leaned in closer to Kurtis, took his hand, and ushered him inside. "You can wait in the living room. No need to take your boots off, the floor is child proof. Do you like marshmallows in your cocoa?"

He hopped on to the large, old-fashioned stuffed sofa, kicked off his rubber Batman boots, and nodded. "Like 'mallows."

"You don't need to do this, Katie. We were just offering to help with the tree—nothing more."

Mark stood in the doorway as if he was afraid to cross the threshold. His lack of confidence surprised her. He'd never been hesitant while she'd known him, and in his line or work, if what everyone said was true, she was sure any hesitation on his part could be deadly.

"No trouble. Like I said, I was about to make a cup for myself after I took care of the tree. Give me a minute to put the water on to heat, and I'll be right back."

Memories of their time together flooded her mind. She held her breath, then shook her head as she made her way to the kitchen. Good Lord, what was she doing? She shouldn't be resurrecting memories from the past. Kurtis' pleading gaze, identical to his fathers, melted her heart. How could she refuse his request for hot cocoa? His trusting hand in hers had her yearning for a child of her own. The one she'd lost. Kurtis was a typical two-year-old—precious. She wanted to wrap him in her arms and hug him to pieces. But he wasn't hers to hug. It would only lead to heartache all over again.

"Not a good idea. Not a good idea. Definitely not a good idea to let Mark Logan back in my house. My life," she muttered under her breath. She filled the tea kettle, set it on the stove, and switched the burner on high. Her vision blurred as she assembled the hot chocolate packets, pulled cups out of the cupboard above the counter, and grabbed the bag of miniature, colored marshmallows. She leaned against the counter. Elvis' sultry voice filtered from the other room as he continued to recount decorations of red and things not being the same without you. The words stabbed her heartstrings. Her first Christmas without Mark had been bad enough. She'd cried herself to sleep countless nights.

The second Christmas hadn't been much better. Now, her mind flitted back to Sven, and she wondered why she wasn't as disappointed as she should be that he wasn't here to help her with the tree, the decorations, instead of Mark and his son. She gripped the countertop, sucked in a deep breath in an effort to try to calm her shaking insides. Her hands were no better. When she ripped open a packet of cocoa mix, half the contents spilled all over the counter top. It was a good thing she had a large supply of mix. She wiped down the counter, sighed, and then headed back to the living room while she waited for the water to boil.

She stopped in the doorway and closed her eyes. *I can do this. I can do this.* When she opened them, she discovered Mark had already brought in the tree, and taken his boots and heavy winter jacket off. A teal wool sweater, a pair of worn, tight blue jeans showed off his lean, but muscular body. His military style haircut was starting to grow out—she'd loved running her fingers through his hair when they'd been dating, when they'd made love. Her fingers itched to do so again. The man had her heart racing overtime.

"Wow," she all but stuttered. "That was fast. You

should have waited for me to help."

"Not a problem. It wasn't heavy. Where do you want me to put it?"

With those muscular biceps, broad chest, and shoulders, she wasn't surprised he didn't feel the strain. He certainly appeared more fit than when he played football back in high school, not to mention drop-dead sexy since she'd seen him last. Those arms—arms that once held her…No! She couldn't go there. She wouldn't.

"Umm, you can center it in front of the window. Give me a minute, and I'll get the tree stand."

Thankfully, the next song on the CD was a recording of "Jingle Bells," sung by someone other than Elvis.

Another escape. But this time, little footsteps followed her down the hallway. She extended her hand behind her back, and wiggled her fingers, an invitation for Kurtis to latch on to them. Kurtis clasped his tiny fingers around hers; his touch warmed her insides. She smiled as she quietly led him toward the hall closet where she opened the door, dug among the many containers of scarves, mitten, hats, and an assortment of odds and ends, until she uncovered the tree stand way in the back.

"Here." She squatted to his level and held the stand out to him. "Do you think you can help me carry this back to your father?"

"Me help." He nodded, his fine dark hair flying forward, his wide-eyed grin tugged at her heart as he grabbed one of the green metal legs. He tucked it in toward his tummy, swiveled, and then ran as fast as his little legs could carry him all the way back to the front room.

"Ho, ho, ho. I see you have a helper," Mark chuckled.

The sound of Mark's ho, ho, ho washed over her like a tsunami. She froze. His eyes twinkled and gazed into hers, his smile beaming. She felt like a reindeer caught in strobing police headlights. Oh. My. God! Santa? Mark's ho, ho, ho sounded an awful lot like the lodge's Santa's ho, ho, ho! She gulped. Could it be? Mark? Santa? Was he the one who had played Santa last Sunday? And seen her dressed in that dorky elf outfit? No way! Her body flamed as the blood rushed to her neck, her cheeks, and clear to the roots of her hair, and scorched her insides. Oh, no! Please, no! She gulped again, took the tree stand from Kurtis, studied it like a lifeline, and with eyes averted, handed it to Mark in silence.

The tea kettle whistled. Oh, crap. She'd forgotten all about the tea kettle and the hot cocoa. She practically ran to the kitchen to escape, saving her from making a complete fool of herself.

Good, Lord. Why hadn't he said something? And why hadn't he gotten in touch with her afterwards? He'd had all week.

Katelyn shut the burner under the kettle off, mixed the cocoa, poured a bit of milk in each cup, and set them on a tray. How could she face Mark in the other room after this unsavory revelation? She turned on the kitchen faucet, ran a cloth under the cold water, wrung it out, and pressed it to her face. Why had she ever let her father talk her into playing an elf? Never mind inviting Mark in to help with the tree—him and his son. It was too late—the only thing she could do now was go back in there, face him and hope he wasn't still laughing at seeing her in that ridiculous elf outfit.

She returned to the front room carrying the tray of warm, steaming cups of cocoa, and a dish of pumpkin sugar cookies her mother had sent home with her the night before. The aroma of warm chocolate, sugar, vanilla, and spiced pumpkin filled the room. Mark was on his knees trying to pacify Kurtis, who had gone from a smiling kid to a distraught, sulking, almost in tears unhappy tot standing straight in defiance, his lips pursed, challenging his father. She hated to see Kurtis upset when they had been enjoying a special holiday moment.

"Can I help?" Katelyn set the tray on the coffee table. The look in Mark's eyes almost silenced her, but she loved kids, was comfortable around them, and wanted to resolve whatever issue was causing such conflict between the two. Perhaps a distraction would help.

"Anyone up for Christmas cookies to go with cocoa?"

Kurtis eyed her, and then looked back at his father as if trying to decide how far he could push his father's buttons to find out what he could get away with without dire repercussions. Typical two-year-old. He frowned, waiting for Mark to give him the go ahead. Mark finally nodded his assent. Only then did Kurtis slowly walk over to Katelyn and ask for a cookie. She wanted to pick him up and hug his cuteness, but knew better than to pit father against son. Instead, she handed Kurtis the smaller mug of coca, and a cookie on a red Christmas napkin.

"Let's sit on the floor next to the fire to enjoy our

cocoa," she said, leading the way.

Kurtis plunked down as if nothing had transpired between him and Mark, and bit into a cookie. With Kurtis occupied with his snack, Katelyn could hold her tongue no longer.

"What was that all about?" she asked over the top of Kurtis' head.

"He wanted to help you decorate the tree. I told him we've imposed enough. We only planned to help you bring the tree in the house, and set it up. In his own words, he insisted that meant decorating it, too."

"He's such a sweet boy, Mark. You should be proud he wants to help others. I can get the decorations from the attic. Of course, he can help."

"Katie—"

"Done deal. Unless you have someplace else to be?" What the hell was she thinking? The sooner he left, the sooner she could address her own confused melancholy emotions, and decorate her own tree—and sit and sulk alone.

"You don't have to do this. He's only two. No need to cater to him. You don't know the kid like I do. Once you give in, it's never ending. He'll have you wrapped around your finger in no time."

Katelyn laughed. "Too late. I think he already has. Come on, Mark, it'll be fun to have a little kid help me decorate. What's Christmas for, if not to get pleasure in watching children enjoy and share the excitement of the Christmas season?"

Was she making herself miserable on purpose? Having Kurtis here—Mark's son…

As if to emphasize her words, the music on the CD switched to "Have Yourself a Merry Little Christmas."

She smiled, and became mesmerized when Mark's solemn expression turned upside down—his grin stirred memories better left tucked away.

"Finish your hot cocoa while I get the decorations." She stood and placed her cup on the tray. Mark followed suit.

"Let me help. If I know you, there'll be several boxes."

Katelyn was aware of every movement Mark made as he followed her up the stairs to the second floor, and then down the hallway to the attic door. Her grandmother had insisted a regular stairway be put in to make it easier to access the attic. Visions of having to climb a ladder to squeeze through a square hole in the ceiling, like most of the older New England homes sported, had her thankful for her grandmother's foresight. Otherwise, she would never have contemplated using the attic to store her decorations. Or anything else.

The door wasn't locked, and opened easily. A cold draft of winter air whooshed down the stairs and into the hall, blowing at Katelyn's hair.

"I forgot how cold and damp Maine winters could be," Mark said. "I hope we don't have to rummage around up here too long."

"Everything should be just to the left at the top of the stairs. I try to keep things as organized as possible. Makes it easier to retrieve when I need something. Not that there's much to rummage through."

Mark climbed the stairs, ducked so his head wouldn't bump into the rafters, and made his way to the center of the dark space where he was able to stand.

"There should be a pull-string for the light right

about where you're standing."

"Got it."

She heard the click of the string attached to a single fifty-watt bulb that hung from the rafters, and was relieved that the bulb hadn't blown as the attic became illuminated.

"Wow! This is the neatest attic I've ever seen."

"Not much to clutter. Mom and Dad took care of most of my grandparents' things after they died. There are a few boxes with items they saved for nostalgia purposes, and then a few of my own things from my childhood I can't seem to part with. I keep them labeled so I know what's in the boxes."

Katelyn climbed the last two steps and joined Mark. Despite the cold air, the body heat from Mark's closeness in the small space was intoxicating. Still, she wrapped her hands around her arms and rubbed them.

"Here"—she pointed—"these containers are the decorations." Four bright red plastic containers with green lids were stacked neatly to the left.

"You're freezing. Wait at the bottom, and I'll hand these to you."

Katelyn didn't hesitate. Not only did she want to get out of the frigid space, she needed to put space between her and Mark.

Together they lugged the containers full of decorations to the living room. When the last one was down, they found Kurtis trying to open one, a devilish, cookie crumb and cocoa mustachioed smile on his inquisitive face. He stopped in his attempt, and looked up at Katelyn in anticipation. Once again her heart melted. She had all to do not to lift him into her arms and squeeze him. Instead, she took his hand and drew him toward a container full of ornaments he was sure to enjoy. She helped him open the lid.

"Let's start with this one. You choose any of these bulbs or decorations to put on the tree. You can put it wherever you think it would look best." The box was sectioned off with small Disney ornaments her parents and grandparents had given her each year for Christmas. All the princesses where there, as well as the Mickey Mouse clan. She figured Kurtis would like them best, and handed him a couple to start putting on the branches.

"What about the lights and garland? Are you sure you want him to load the tree with bulbs first, only to have to reassemble everything later?"

"Hush your mouth. Why, these decorations will stay right where Kurtis puts them." She gave him what she hoped was a conspiratorial smile, and winked. "Besides, we can work around anything he's able to get hung before we finish stringing the lights. Somehow I don't see him sitting quietly aside while we work on the lights. As for the garland, I gave up on that a long time ago. Never been able to get it exactly where I want it to go. It just seems to hang there looking all loopy and pathetic."

"We can't have loopy, now can we? So, which box has the string of lights?"

After checking to make sure each strand was in working order, Mark helped her string the lights around the tree, stepping around Kurtis, who had at least two ornaments on each branch along the very bottom of the tree. Katelyn held the string of lights, while Mark placed them in among the branches. Their shoulders bumped into each other, their hands touched, and the scent of the pine mingled with memories of earlier days. A smile, a laugh, the sight of Mark and Kurtis in her home, as if they were family, had warmth washing over her clear to her toes. What would life be like if Mark hadn't gone away? Would they be together now? Like this? Would they have had other children?

She turned, stepped away from the tree, sniffed back a tear, and hated herself for getting emotional. It had to be the season. Or the sight of Mark again, with his son, igniting memories she thought buried forever.

Mark plugged in the lights. Although she hadn't finished decorating the house yet, the sparkling colors from the tree brightened the room. Kurtis had curled up on the sofa, his head resting against one of the plush pillows, his eyes drooping. The latest Christmas CD clicked off, and like a dose of reality, Katelyn's festive mood disappeared with the awkward silence.

"I think that's my signal which proves we've overstayed our visit. Kurtis will be hungry as a bear if I don't get him home soon." Mark stood and went to his son's side. "Time to go, bud."

Kurtis didn't fuss—he willingly sat up, his head lolling sideways.

Having Mark and Kurtis share these special moments was bittersweet. She couldn't be drawn into Mark and Kurtis' lives. She had to remember that this was a one-time occurrence.

"Thanks so much for your help this morning," she said, bending to snap a lid on one of the now empty containers. "I loved having someone share the fun."

"Thank you, Katie. Kurtis really enjoyed it. It hasn't been easy for him, losing his mother at such an early age. I'm hoping this Christmas will be a special one for him. You've given us the opportunity to get the ball rolling in the right direction."

Katelyn didn't know the story behind Mark's wife and her death, but now wasn't the time to enquire. However, it didn't stop her heart from aching for Kurtis. Just thinking about a motherless child at Christmastime broke her heart. Not to mention a childless mother. A knot twisted inside—she knew all too well the desolate ache of losing a child. Even an unborn one.

Katelyn started picking up the remaining ornaments and tucked them back in one of the empty containers. Mark walked to the sofa, lifted Kurtis onto his lap and proceeded to put on his son's boots.

"Come on, bud. Let's get your coat on and get you home before you fall asleep."

Mark carried Kurtis to the front door, set him on the floor and helped him on with his outerwear. Katelyn followed. About to say goodbye, Mark startled her when he swept her into his arms and kissed her smack on the lips. His long, lingering kiss threw her into a tailspin of remembered passions. Before she could wrap her arms around his neck and sink into his embrace, he let her go.

Stunned, Katelyn could only stare as a hot, searing heat of embarrassment washed over her.

"I've wanted to do that since you walked in the lodge dining room wearing that sexy elf outfit last Sunday. I know you're engaged, but I'm not going to apologize for that kiss. This has been the best home-coming I've ever had. Thank you, Katie, for letting us come into your home."

Oh, my God! This was her worst nightmare. "That

was you! You *were* the one who played Sant—oops!" She looked at Kurtis, hoping he hadn't figured out what she had been about to disclose. "Why didn't you say something? You kept staring at me all morning—I looked like a freak in that get-up."

"Definitely not a freak. I'm sure you turned a few heads, including mine. It was hard to concentrate on the kids with you in the room. You have a unique flair with kids, by the way."

"Up, up," Kurtis cried, his arms flung out to his father before Katelyn could respond. Mark lifted him into his arms, gave Katelyn a quick peck on the cheek, and turned to leave.

"Me kiss Katie."

Kurtis leaned toward Katelyn. If Kurtis caused her heart to melt any more, there would be nothing left but a puddle in the middle of the floor. She gave him access to her cheek, surprised when he wrapped his arms around her neck and gave her a tight hug, too.

"He's not so shy about what he wants. Guess adults could learn a thing or two from kids."

Katelyn didn't have a comeback. What was Mark trying to say?

"Thanks for letting Kurtis stay to help decorate." Mark opened the door and stepped out on the front porch. A blast of cold air filled the space between them, yet Katelyn didn't feel the bitter temperature.

"I enjoyed having him help. Thanks."

Before Mark's car pulled out of the drive, Katelyn shut the front door, scuffed across the floor, and plunked down on the sofa. What the hell just happened? Dear Lord, she was in trouble. Her heart was full— fuller than it had been in a very long time. And she had no business letting Mark and Kurtis have such an all-consuming impact on her so soon after seeing him again. She had thought that part of her life was over—that she'd let the past go. But his kiss, however short-lived, had curled her toes. And brought back bittersweet memories.

She gazed around the room at the disarray of the remaining Christmas decorations—tissue papers, ribbon, and leftover lights—not really seeing any of it. She sat, stunned at her behavior. His kiss had taken her back to their high school love and the feelings they had once shared. Six years ago, to be exact. Still hot from the internal combustion to her heart from his kiss, she covered her face with her hands, threw herself sideways on the sofa, buried her head in the pillows, and let out a loud groan, thankfully disguised as a moan, in the depths of the fluffy material.

She sat up, shook her head. For God's sake, she was engaged. Why was she acting as if Mark had just walked back into her life and she was welcoming him with open arms? She couldn't let that happen. Couldn't let Kurtis grow too fond of her. She couldn't grow too fond of Kurtis. They would both be hurt when Mark found someone else to fill his dead wife's shoes. There were plenty of single women in Lobster Cove for him to choose from, but finding someone to be a mother for Kurtis…well…she hoped he chose wisely.

Her thoughts were way out of control—it was only a kiss between old lovers—a high school infatuation. She was putting too much into that kiss. She had to get a grip!

She wiped her hands over her face, took a deep breath, and allowed herself one final reflection in

48

regards to Mark—why did she still have feelings for him when she was engaged to Sven?

OMG! Sven!

Chapter Four

Sven!

Katelyn stepped around the half decorated tree, pulled the drapes away from the window, and took a moment to observe the lazy snowflakes drifting down outside. The trees were dusted white—the sidewalks would need shoveling soon. Sven wasn't here to shovel them for her, something he always insisted on doing. Such a gentleman, worrying about her—taking good care of her. How could she forget about him so easily?

She'd been so overwhelmed with Mark and Kurtis helping her decorate, she'd forgotten about Sven. She recalled the conversation she'd had with Sven the day before he left for Norway—and tried hard to find the perfect, long-lasting connection between them.

"I'll be home for Christmas," Sven had said when he'd stopped by to say goodbye Thursday night before Breakfast with Santa. "Perhaps I'll let you talk me into a wedding date when I return." He had given her a quick kiss on her cheek. His smile had promised a boat load of happiness, and she'd smiled back, thinking to hold him to that promise—it would make a great Christmas present.

"You sound like a Christmas song," she'd told him. "I wish you didn't have to leave during my most favorite time of year. You're going to miss Christmas caroling at the park. I'm going to miss you." She'd snuggled against him, ecstatic at the thought of finally setting a date.

"It's the grandparents' fiftieth anniversary—I can't get out of it. Mom said they've made special holiday arrangements with the rest of the family and friends. I don't want to disappoint everyone." He put her at arm's length and gazed into her eyes. His remorseful expression made her feel guilty. She'd almost wished he'd stay in Lobster Cove with her and miss his grandparents' celebration.

She'd latched on to his shirt collar, pulled him close, and planted a kiss on his lips. "We'll talk about a lot more than dates when you return. Tell your grandparents happy anniversary for me. I can't wait to meet them one day."

He'd wound his arms around her in a tight embrace, and kissed her again, then set her aside, kissed her forehead, and walked to the door. He swung it open, letting in a stiff cold breeze. Her empty, aching arms had hung at her sides. Katelyn had grabbed a sweater from the back of the chair in the hallway and wrapped it around her chilled body to ward off the cold from outside. A sudden emptiness assailed her. He hadn't asked her to join him—a bit of a letdown, she had to admit. But then, being realistic, she did have a few more days of classes to complete before the end of the semester, and then there was her work program at Hearts and Hands Daycare. She shouldn't have been so disappointed she hadn't gotten an invitation to go to Norway with him. But she was. She had waved at Sven's retreating tail lights, shut the front door, and leaned against it as disappointment overshadowed the start of the Christmas holiday she'd been looking forward to celebrating. With Sven.

She convinced herself he wasn't going to be gone forever. He had promised he'd be home in time to spend Christmas week with her. Besides, they would have plenty of other opportunities to visit his family in Norway after they were married. And who knew, they might even have their own little Olson to show off when they did visit.

Looking back at their conversation caused doubts to set in. Doubts she wasn't ready to deal with. She was being silly trying to read something into Sven's goodbye that wasn't there. Thinking back, his kisses hadn't affected her in the same way as Mark's kiss had today. And she didn't want to think about why that was—or why it should matter.

She gazed in amazement at the beginnings of the spirit of Christmas now filling her living room. No more moping about, she had things to do. She pulled out decorations and started arranging them around the room. She found the new red and green candles she bought the other day and displayed them on the end tables next to the sofa, surrounding them with plastic holly wreathes. She found her childhood stocking her grandmother had knitted for her, with her name on it, and hung it on the side of the fireplace. Next she unearthed her grandmother's Christmas village, and arranged that on the mantel. She wasn't finished yet, but it was a start. Feeling much better, and infused with the Christmas spirit once again, she went to the back porch and retrieved the clippings from the lower branches of the tree Mark had snipped off, and arranged them in a wreath for the front door. Pleased with her attempts, she quickly tidied up the remainder of the boxes of decorations littered around the floor in the front room.

Katelyn took a moment to freshen her makeup, comb her hair, and then headed to Mariner's earlier than planned. Her parents would need help with the dinner crowd. Her mother would already have decorated the restaurant from top to bottom with greens, miniature stuffed red lobsters, silver and gold bells hanging from the rafters, and red and green candles set in the center of holly with red berries on each table. There would be plenty of people from the community in the holiday spirit to mingle with and help get her mind off Sven's absence.

And Mark's kisses.

****

Mark had strapped Kurtis in his car seat, and then buckled his own seatbelt before starting the car and backing out of Katelyn's driveway. He hadn't lied—seeing her in that elf outfit, and then spending the day helping her decorate her tree, was the best welcome home he could have asked for—for both him and Kurtis. Sure, his parents had met him at the airport, tears, smiles, hugs, and kisses, and he had been filled with love. He hadn't realized how much he had missed them, and what it meant to them to have him home—to see their grandson for the first time. He almost cried when his mother took Kurtis in her arms, tears of happiness flowing down her pale cheeks. Having a child of his own now, he understood those emotions. He silently chastised himself for letting this homecoming be so long in coming.

And he hadn't lied when he'd told Katie how he felt about seeing her again after all this time. He had meant it when he said her interactions with the kids and adults at Breakfast with Santa was a gift to the community. The way she had treated Kurtis was special, too. She'd make a great mother.

He stopped at the intersection, turned left, and with a jolt, grasped the fact that her children would be someone else's—not his. They would belong to this Sven person—the man she was engaged to.

Why should that bother him? He didn't know, but it did. He no longer had a hold on Katie's heart. He'd given that up years ago. He'd been an ass to not keep in touch, to have cut the ties so completely. He was surprised she'd even given him the time of day today, after the way he had practically ignored her all these years. Shit. If he were her, he wouldn't be so forgiving. The woman had the heart of a saint. She hadn't even acted as if he'd broken her heart. Had he? Was she being a trouper and holding it all in? Damn. Maybe he should apologize—clear the air. Fill her in on what he'd been through, why he hadn't wanted to drag her into the kind of life he'd led. Even though she was engaged, he felt the need to come clean and hope she'd understand. After spending time with her today, he was pretty sure she'd forgive him. At least he hoped so.

He pulled into his parents' driveway, turned the ignition off, and helped Kurtis out of the car seat.

"Come on, bud. Let's get you inside and see what Grandma has for lunch. I'll get Grandpa Logan to help with the tree. After you have something to eat and have a nap, we'll get working on decorating our own tree. Whaddya say?"

Kurtis nodded his head and laid it against Mark's shoulder. God, he loved this little guy—something he was surprised to realize shortly after he'd been born. What would it be like had he and Katie had children? His insides warmed. Then sobered. It was too late. She was engaged. Whether she forgave him or not, she had found love in someone else's arms.

As had he.

****

The Bergen hotel banquet hall was full to overflowing with family, friends, and waiters circling the room with serving trays laden with hors d'oeuvres and champagne. Sven wound his way through the crowd until he reached his grandfather's side. His grandfather stood in front of the head table, talking to a plump elderly woman dressed in a typical Norwegian wool sweater, long skirt, and sturdy brown strapped shoes, her back to the crowded room. His grandfather made a striking figure, leaning on his cane, with his trimmed white hair, black tux, and polished shoes. Sven drew alongside him, waiting politely for his grandfather to finish his conversation being conducted in Norwegian.

"Sven, you remember Aunt Olga?" His grandfather finally acknowledged him.

He hadn't seen his aunt in years and hadn't recognized her.

"Of course he does. Come here, you." Aunt Olga pulled him in for a huge hug. "Such a good boy to come to help celebrate your grandparent's special occasion. Are you moving back with your mother and father to help with the family business here in Bergen?"

What? What was she talking about? Was she getting more befuddled in her older years? Sven returned her hug, and then stepped back, turned to his grandfather, eyebrows raised.

"Now, Olga, I don't think that's public knowledge just yet." His grandfather coughed and held his chest as he scolded her.

What the hell was going on here? His parents hadn't mentioned a thing about moving back to Norway. Why were they moving back to Bergen? And when had this all come about? And if true, when were they going to tell him?

"I can see Sven is unaware. Now son, don't worry. Things aren't final. They're just thinking about it."

His grandfather's tone was raspy. He hadn't detected it earlier, but it was obvious something was wrong.

"You have caught me by surprise, *Bestefar.* I can see I need to talk to Father and find out what is going on. If you'll excuse me."

"See what you've done, Olga." His grandfather chastised his aunt.

Sven turned on a dime and made his way through the crowded hotel banquet hall in search of his father. He spotted him leaning against the far wall, a tall glass of champagne in his hand, talking to an equally tall, heavy-set man he didn't recognize. Both looked to be involved in a serious discussion. Sven could only surmise it had something to do with their intended relocation to Norway. He slowed, and was about to turn away and search out his mother instead, when his father spotted him, and motioned him forward.

"Hello, son. Let me introduce you to Mr. Christenssen. Hans, this is my son, Sven."

Sven extended his hand in greeting. The man nodded, his grip firm, as he returned the handshake.

"Hans and I were just discussing a proposition which might include you, if you wish."

"What's going on Dad? Aunt Olga mentioned something about moving back home to Bergen. What's that all about?"

He didn't mean to be rude, but he couldn't hide his displeasure at not being part of the decision-making process in the first place. He shoved his shaking hands in his pockets, stood erect, his silently raised eyebrows demanding an explanation. After all, he worked for his parents and was part of their Flowers in Bloom flower shop back in Lobster Cove. What was behind this decision that had left him out of that process? And what was going to happen to him—and the Flowers in Bloom business?

"Yes, well, Aunt Olga has been talking to your mother, and you know your aunt doesn't know how or when to keep her mouth shut. She can twist things around to her own way of thinking." His father smiled, plucked a tiny lobster hors d'oeuvre from a passing platter and popped it in his mouth. Sven waited impatiently for him to swallow.

The lobster reminded him of Lobster Cove, and Katelyn. And how this news was going to affect her—them. He wasn't amused—far from it. Yes, Aunt Olga was a bit of a gossip, but there was always some truth to her tales.

"So why don't you fill me in on what's happening?"

"If you'll excuse me, gentlemen." Mr. Christenssen looked embarrassed, nodded at Sven, then addressed his father. "I can see you two need to have a private word. I'll see you in my office Monday morning at ten o'clock. We'll finalize everything then."

Sven turned to his father the minute Mr. Christenssen was out of hearing range.

"What is going on? Give it to me straight, Dad."

"Let's go somewhere private."

His father led him through a side door away from the buzz of too many conversations going on at the same time, and too many ears. If they needed this much privacy, Sven knew he wasn't going to be happy with the answers his father was about to impart. Just how long had his parents been planning this move?

"Have a seat, son."

Sven waited for his father to sit in one of the low, plush maroon chairs on either side of a round oak tea table covered with an ivory damask tablecloth, and a holiday centerpiece. He sat in the opposite chair and folded his hands in his lap. Several red candles flickered in a circle of green ivy in the center. Sven studied the small flames as they flickered while he waited for his father to speak. When he didn't appear to know where to begin, Sven raised an eyebrow expectantly, met his father's eyes in encouragement—wanting him to share this big family secret so they could discuss it as a family—a family business decision.

"Okay, so, I didn't want to say anything until I was sure of the outcome." His father crossed one leg over the other and folded his hands in his lap—his demeanor was more at ease than Sven's. "I had to come back home to find out for myself which way the wind was blowing."

His father paused as if to find the right words, as if Sven was a child who needed to be talked down to. The strained silence dragged on until Sven could stand it no longer.

"So, which way does the wind blow, Dad?"

"Don't get wise with me. Calm down. Hear me out first."

"Sorry." Scolded, Sven sighed, ran his hand through his hair, over his face, folded them in his lap, and sighed again.

"I know this must be a shock. It was to your mother and me, as well. Your grandfather is very ill—he's had a couple of bad spells before we came home—pneumonia and a TIA they call a mini-stroke. He asked me to come back to Bergen and run the family business. Actually, he's ready to turn the entire franchise over to us. Immediately."

That explained his grandfather's coughing and waxy appearance earlier. He loved his grandfather and had no idea he was so ill. His outward appearance had shown him to be in excellent health. Sven had no idea his illness was bad enough that he had to give up the family business he'd inherited from his father before him.

"But you don't know anything about the fishing business."

"It's a family business. I grew up working in the business. It's been a while, but it was my life for a long time. In fact, it's what took us to the U.S.—to Lobster Cove. The McClintocks hired me when I first arrived. It was your mother who got started in the flower business. She made a success out of it, so I gave up my job on the fishing boats to work with her."

"So now you're giving up everything you worked so hard for in Maine to come back to Bergen and the fishing business?"

"Your mother and I miss Norway. We're not getting any younger, and we want to be closer to our family—to our parents, for however long they have left."

"What about me? What am I supposed to do? Katelyn and I are engaged, we've been talking about a wedding. How am I going to support a wife? A family?"

He sounded ungracious and only concerned for himself. He didn't mean to act quite so petulant. He hung his head, his shoulders. He really should be thinking of his grandparents. His parents. But...

"I'm sorry this is so hard for you to understand. Yes, we've considered your part in the business. We know you have your life ahead of you in America. You'll have to talk to Katelyn and decide what is best for the two of you."

"What about Flowers in Bloom?"

"We would love to turn it over to you, but financially, we can't afford to simply walk away. We need the money to transition to the business here in Bergen, pay things off back in Lobster Cove, and give the fishing business a boost to keep it going. Maybe tie in with McClintock and McClintock Shipping. We'll have to put the business on the market right after the first of the year. Perhaps, if you decide to stay in Lobster Cove, the new owners will hire you to work for them."

Speechless, Sven swallowed the rant bubbling deep inside his gut. He didn't want to disrespect his father, or grandfather. But, damn it, he lived above the flower shop with his parents. Where was he to go once they sold his home out from under him? What was he going to do? The flower shop was all he'd trained for, all these years. During and after high school he'd only ever worked for his parents. He'd expected one day to become a partner in the business—to own it. It was a successful business, after all. He shook his head, pursed his lips, stood, and walked out of the claustrophobic room.

How had his life gone so terribly wrong, so quickly? How could he marry Katelyn without any financial prospects back in Lobster Cove? No way was he going to have a wife support him.

No way!

He strode down the narrow hall, mindless of his father calling him back. He couldn't talk to him right now, without causing a row. He'd more than likely say things he'd be sorry for later. Once he entered the banquet hall, he was sorry he hadn't turned left and kept right on going straight out of the hotel. The noise and people surrounded him, his head reeled, ready to explode. He shut his eyes, took a deep breath, and crashed into another body, apparently also anxious to leave the hubbub behind.

"I'm so sorry. I wasn't watching where I was going."

"Why, hello, Sven. Fancy bumping into you— literally. Long time, no see."

Before he could respond, Marta Sigurd flung her arms around his neck and plastered her lips against his in a firm embrace that had him backing up to keep from falling on his behind. He wound his arms around her in order to remain upright while the kiss continued. The kiss somehow, without warning, turned more amorous than expected. She leaned into him as if they were the only two in the foyer, igniting memories of how close the two of them had become over the years during his many visits to Norway. Memories of her body being closer than their current embrace. Naked. Making love. Memories better left buried in the past. After all, he was engaged to Katelyn.

Sven slowly regained control of the shock of the intimacy of her hold on him. He ran his hands along her arms, firmly gripped them, and stepped away from her seductive embrace. His strong emotions toward her had to be nothing more than his reaction over his angst with his father. He had to set the record straight.

"That was quite a welcome, Marta. I almost didn't recognize you. You've grown into quite a woman since I saw you last. Guess I don't need to ask how you've been?"

Her blonde hair hung in a thick braid down the middle of her back, her blue eyes wide and mesmerizing. And man, in two years she had filled out and grown into a beautiful woman.

"Well, I had no trouble recognizing you, Sven. You're looking as handsome as ever." Her smile intimated so much more. Sven gulped as his childhood flame continued. "I was hoping to run into you tonight. Guess I did. Let's go someplace and reminisce over old times." She linked her arms through his and started to lead him toward the exit.

"Not a good idea, Marta. I'm engaged to someone back in Maine."

"I only have talk in mind, Sven." Her look told a different story. "Come on. Let me reacquaint you with Bergen. I'll buy you a drink at our old hangout on

Torget Street—for old time's sake. Besides, no one will miss us here."

He drank in her piercing stare—a dare if ever there was one. Hell. Why not? He needed to get away from his father, his family, the overly happy crowd, and clear his mind so he could think. Contemplate what he was going to do now that his entire life had been turned upside down? He let Marta link her arm with his and allowed her to lead him through the throng of celebrants hanging out near the reception area. They retrieved their coats before they exited the hotel and walked briskly against the cold evening air drifting off the harbor along the *Bryggen* District, and made their way to the Irish pub that had become their favorite hangout.

The bar's dark polished wooden interior brought back memories of their time spent together the last time he'd been in Bergen. The tables along the far wall next to the windows were full to overflowing. The lighting dim and welcoming, the live band was already setting the mood, with their jazzy tunes slow and sultry. Marta waved to the bartender, who smiled and waved back, an indication she still frequented the lively establishment. She led Sven to an empty table in a back corner.

"More privacy over here." She smiled over her shoulder, bidding him to follow.

They'd no sooner sat than a waiter was at their table, taking their order.

"The place hasn't changed." Sven sat back and scanned the bar. It was an entertaining hangout for those who enjoyed dancing or just socializing. Before long the dance floor would be put to good use. Couples would be draped around each other as the band catered to the regulars. He and Marta had been part of the dance crowd. Maybe this wasn't such a good idea after all. Maybe he should cut his losses now and leave.

In the midst of contemplating what he should do, their drinks arrived. Marta swirled the straw in her tall, frothy glass, gave him a simpering expression out of the corner of her eye, and then swiped the straw across her tongue with a seductive come-hither motion. Her full red lips slowly sucked the long piece of plastic suggestively before pointing it at his chest. "I've missed coming to this pub with you since the two of us said goodbye and you flitted off to America. You broke my heart, Sven. Remember our special night?"

How could he forget? They'd spent the night together on her father's sailboat out in the fjords. They hadn't gotten far before they'd pulled into a small bay and moored for the night. It had been warm and balmy, the moon shining off the water. Marta's skin was silky smooth and hot, and had driven him to heights he'd had a hard time climbing back down from in the morning. She was looking at him the same way now, and damn, it was going to be hard to withstand her sexy smile, her sexy body, all over again.

"That was a long time ago, Marta. We're different people now. I have a fiancée back home. I'm only going to be here a few more days. Then I'm going back to Maine for Christmas."

"Not what I heard. I understand your parents are moving back to Bergen to run your grandfather's salmon business. Aren't you moving back with your parents to help run the business?"

"Good question. One I haven't had a chance to really think about. I just found out about it tonight. I'm not sure what I'm going to do. I've hardly had time to let it sink in, let alone try to figure out how I fit into their plans. Or if I want to."

"In the meantime, dance with me for old time's sake. Maybe it'll help you figure things out." She sucked on her straw, licked it all the while gazing straight into his eyes, and then set her glass on the table. "Come on, Sven. You owe me a dance for walking out on me."

She stood, grabbed his hand, pulled him to his feet, and led him to the dance floor. He didn't resist. The small space was already crowded with couples wrapped around each other, slow dancing to a lilting melody he didn't recognize. It didn't really matter what song the band played, the minute she splayed herself around him like hot syrup, his mind shut down. She still fit in his arms comfortably, warm, seductively, sending out a message that stirred memories. His problems disappeared. She nuzzled his neck. He swallowed, shifted with the music and leaned his head on hers. Her hair now flowing freely down her back was as soft as spun silk. He ran his hand through it, absently stroking it like a worry bead. He didn't resist when she stood on her tiptoes and kissed him on the mouth with such abandoned passion, his response was instantaneous. The music swirled around them. Her dress was, well, for a hot sultry night it would be just right—hot. But in the middle of a cold Norwegian winter, she must be freezing with the off the shoulder scrap of a dress barely covering her well-endowed breasts. Breasts plastered seductively against his chest. Clothes, or no clothes, he couldn't hold in the groan, and the warmth radiating to his lower extremities. Not only was the dress hot, Marta was hotter than hell since he'd seen her last.

"You haven't changed at all," he whispered in her ear. "Still the same sexy siren I remember."

"Oh, Sven, you still say the most romantic things. I only ever cried out for you."

"I'm engaged, Marta. You'll need to rein in those pheromones. They won't work on me."

"Liar. I can feel what you're feeling. Besides, you're only engaged, not married."

"Soon to be."

"But not. Let's get us another drink. We still have a lot of catching up to do."

Sven had no option but to escort her off the dance floor. Removing her arm from around him was a feeble attempt at best. She clung, as if he would escape in a puff of smoke. He let out the breath he didn't realize he'd been holding. For his own sanity and peace of mind, he should walk away. Only three more days left in Bergen, and then he'd be going back home to Lobster Cove.

And Katelyn.

Chapter Five

Katelyn drove past the park along the harbor on her way to St. Joseph's Church Sunday morning. Garlands swung across the streets around the square, the gold and red bells nestled inside the fresh green wreaths hanging at each electric pole. The morning air was tranquil, a light haze swirled up from the bay. The town square gazebo decked from top to bottom displayed large red plastic bows and evergreens festooned around the railings. From the top of the McClintocks warehouse next to Pier One, a humongous wreath welcomed in the season and the people of Lobster Cove. Eugenia McClintock, although no longer in control of the business, would be appreciative to learn they had continued her traditions. Each of the trawlers docked along the pier was also decked out for the holiday, with a string of lights lit from stem to stern.

Other businesses along the drive were likewise dressed for the season. Store fronts were decorated in reds, greens, and golds, and lights all aglow, even on a Sunday. Katelyn rounded the corner of Main and Maple. Whoever was keeping things going at Flowers in Bloom, while Sven and his parents were in Norway, had made sure the store front was looking as seasonally colorful and festive as ever.

Flowers in Bloom reminded her of the Olsons—and Sven. Celebrating the season alone wasn't what she'd envisioned once they had become engaged. They were an official couple now—going to holiday events alone took the enjoyment out of everything.

When was Sven coming home?

As she pulled into the church parking lot, the mist cleared and a few rays of sunshine peeked through. The early morning light appeared, encrusting the surrounding trees and rooftops in sparkling ice crystals. Up ahead, couples and families entered the church ushering their children up the steps. Behind her, another car rushed past to gain an empty space in the parking lot as if they were late to mass. Katelyn took her time, parked, locked the door, and made her way past the life-size crèche in the church's side lawn.

Jeff Myers, the high school P.E. teacher and football coach, greeted her and the other arrivals as they entered and then took their seats. His wife Beth played the organ as Katelyn joined her parents in the Sullivan's usual pew. It wasn't long before the introductory notes of the hymn heralded Father Zack and his followers as they made their way down the center aisle. Katelyn followed the procession with her eyes, and spotted Todd and Lois Logan—and Mark and Kurtis—several pews ahead, on the opposite side of the church. She hadn't paid much attention to the Logan's attendance over the years, and was surprised to see them.

Kurtis sat between Mark and Mrs. Logan.

Father Zack's sermon centered around the essence of the season, and a reminder of those who were in need. Before she realized it, mass had concluded and Father Zack was issuing an invitation to attend coffee hour after the service. She and her parents seldom remained for coffee hour, needing to get back to the restaurant for the lunch crowd, while others, like Helen Troy from the Lobster Cove Grocery Mart, who more than likely provided most of the refreshments, and Coleman Baker and his wife Edna from McClintocks, headed downstairs to the reception hall for the social hour. She followed her parents along the side aisle, wrapped her scarf around her neck, and slipped her gloves on as they entered the vestibule on their way out of church.

Mark, along with Kurtis and his parents approached from behind.

"What's your rush?" Mark's words drew their attention. She and her parents turned as one to greet the Logans.

Katelyn wasn't prepared to meet his sexy smile, his sparkling eyes, and the warmth his nearness had on her insides after the kiss they'd shared yesterday. She busied herself putting on her gloves, and found another pair of eyes, equally as charming as Mark's, looking at her. Kurtis' lips lifted in a wide smile.

"Hi, Katie."

"Hi, yourself. Did you get your tree decorated yesterday?"

"Yes. Grandma let me help."

"Mr. and Mrs. Logan." Dawn Sullivan extended her hand in welcome to Mark's parents. Katelyn's father followed suit, and the four exchanged greetings.

"Mom, Dad, you remember Mark. And this is his son, Kurtis." Kurtis' arm was hung tightly around his father's neck.

"Of course I remember Mark. How you doing, son?" Her father extended his hand in greeting. "And who's this little man you have here?"

"Good to see you again, Mr. Sullivan. Mrs. Sullivan." Mark extended his hand, meeting her father's welcome. "This is my son, Kurtis."

Katelyn smiled at the Logans, who were understandably happy to have their son and grandson home and attending church with them as a family.

"Welcome home to Lobster Cove," her mother greeted Kurtis. "Are you all set for Santa's visit?"

Kurtis smiled, nodded. And tucked his head in Mark's neck. If her heart didn't stop turning over at every move Kurtis made, she was going cave in and make a fool of herself. Knowing he was Mark's son had her insides shaking, thinking about the son she had lost.

"Katelyn, I understand you had a little helper the other day." Lois Logan filled in the awkward pause in conversation.

"Yes," she breathed. "I enjoyed having Kurtis help decorate my tree. He's such an enthusiastic helper."

"Katelyn loves children," her mother interjected as if it was of upmost importance for the Logans to know. "She's getting her degree in childhood development come spring. She works part time at the Hearts and Hand Daycare, too."

"How wonderful you've continued your studies. You'll have to come for dinner sometime soon so we can catch up," Mrs. Logan invited. "In fact, why not come this afternoon?"

"Thank you, but I usually help out at Mariner's for the Sunday after church crowd."

"Nonsense," her father chided. "I'm sure we can manage one afternoon without you. You've worked so hard lately, you deserve a break. Besides, we aren't busy at the moment."

Katelyn knew better. She wasn't sure what her father was thinking—why he was encouraging her to go. She wanted no part of it. Especially when she happened to catch Mark's grin and raised eyebrows.

"Go, Katie girl," her father prodded. "You work too hard. It's time to relax a bit. Get out. Enjoy."

"It's settled. We'll see you at one o'clock," Todd Logan said, ushering his wife down the church steps.

"It's very kind of you to offer, thanks. Can I bring anything?"

"Oh, my goodness, no. Just come and relax. It will be like old times." Mrs. Logan's warm smile lit up her face.

The congregation dispersed around them as those not staying for coffee headed toward their individual vehicles.

Mark lagged behind, his lips lifted as if he had something to say, but just nodded and headed to his car with Kurtis. His silence puzzled her. He hadn't said a word one way or the other, but the smile on his face was disconcerting. Was he responsible for his mother issuing the invitation? After their parting kiss yesterday, she wasn't so sure it was a good idea to spend more time with him and his son—or his family. But how could she refuse after her father had dismissed needing her at the restaurant so persuasively? What was up with that?

Kurtis had suddenly demanded Mark's attention, so Katelyn had no idea what Mark was thinking in regards to his mother's invitation. Should she call out to them and tell them she'd changed her mind? She wanted to, but then Mark looked back at her, and smiled—again. Her heart fluttered when she spotted his sexy dimple.

Once again she couldn't resist the challenge.

****

Katelyn pulled her small car into the Logans' driveway. The home was a simple New England style cottage, small but cozy. She took a deep breath, put the car in park, turned the ignition off, and stepped out into the cold afternoon. She shivered and drew her scarf around her neck, glad she'd worn her heavier wrap. The damp air could chill to the bone, despite the sun overhead. One needed to be hearty in order to live so close to the East Coast.

Before she could knock on the door, Mrs. Logan had it open, welcoming her with a warm, but hesitant hug. She returned the sincere gesture.

"It's so nice to have you visit again, Katelyn. It's been a long time. Come on in."

"Thank you, Mrs. Logan."

"Please, call me Lois. Let me take your wrap. We're almost ready to sit down. The men are in the sitting room."

Both Mark and his father stood as she joined them. Kurtis, standing next to his father, appeared ready to run to her, but held back. Her heart thumped—what would it be like to have a child—her child—run to her arms the minute she entered a room?

"So," Mark interrupted her musings, "shall we eat? I think Kurtis isn't going to last much longer."

"I'm sorry if I held things up."

"No, no, my dear." Lois gripped her hands in front of her chest. "You're right on time."

The dining room was no bigger than an eight by ten square foot room, accommodating only a handful of people—a glass china closet and a dry sink filled the corners. An assortment of framed family photographs covered the walls. Mark had no brothers or sisters, so the pictures were mostly of him at various stages of his life. Katelyn noticed that there were none of Kurtis, and figured that would be taken care of before long, now that he was home.

Concerned she'd be uncomfortable visiting the Logans, Todd and Lois made her feel welcome and kept the conversation flowing with general topics. If anything, it was Mark who made her uncomfortable as his piercing eyes and sexy grin kept watch—her knees went weak and shook under the table. She put her hands over her knees in an effort to control the spasms, but it was no use. Kurtis, bless his heart, inched his chair closer to hers so he could sit next to her while he sat quietly and ate. The boy had superb table manners for a two-year-old.

"So, Katelyn, I understand you're about to finish your degree next spring. You must be very pleased." Lois wiped her lips with the pink linen napkin, and laid it back in her lap.

"Thank you, yes. I'm looking forward to finishing in May. I'm hoping to obtain a teaching position. It would be nice if something became available at the elementary school here in Lobster Cove. I plan to put in an application just in case."

"That's wonderful. But what will the daycare do without you?" Todd asked.

"Honestly, it will be hard to leave. But it was a work study project for credit—not a permanent position. I'll need to find something with a decent salary and benefits."

"Once you and your fiancé are married, you might

not want a fulltime position." Mark scooped a fork full of chicken and biscuits into his mouth. His eyes focused on hers.

"I've been looking forward to teaching since I graduated from high school. Still am. What about you, Mark? You haven't said what you plan to do now that you're home? Or are you only here for a visit?"

Silence circled the table. Todd and Lois exchanged looks with Mark—his look guarded. Mrs. Logan concentrated on her half-empty plate. Mr. Logan cleared his throat. Had she said something wrong? Had she unknowingly stepped into a family issue?

"I haven't made up my mind yet," Mark finally answered. "My main focus right now is to settle Kurtis in the community. Make sure it's a pleasant and safe fit for him before I decide on something permanent. As you probably know, I'm planning to register him at Hearts and Hands Daycare. What can you tell me about it?"

A safe topic for sure. Linda Claussen had mentioned he was thinking about registering Kurtis.

"It's an excellent facility. The people who run it are very caring. Each child is not only dealt with on an individual basis, but they are encouraged to work together in groups. Some of the children come from single parent homes. Most of them don't have brothers or sisters, so it's an opportunity for them to interact with others their age. I think it would be a perfect fit for Kurtis. It's a good option. Have you talked to anyone there yet?" As if she didn't know he had.

"Yes. But seeing as you work there, I thought I'd get your opinion."

"Did you know Mark has looked at the McClintock

estate? Seems it's for sale." Todd laid his napkin next to his plate, then drank heartily from his water glass.

Lois wiped her mouth with her napkin, again. It appeared to be a nervous habit. "Now Todd, you know the estate is too large and way too fancy for the likes of us. I'm sure Mark wants something more suitable for a small family. Isn't that right, son?"

"Yes." Mark appeased his mother. He had forgotten how protective and a bit manipulative she was when it came to her family. While her smothering him used to irk him as a child, and especially in his teens, he appreciated her ability to provide and protect her grandson now. "The house is much too ostentatious for the two of us. I'd rather find a fixer-upper—make it ours. I've contacted Jessica Martin's real estate for help."

He turned to his father, wanting to get away from the subject of him and his son and house hunting. He wasn't ready to share details of his job, or his son's safety with anyone at the moment. Even Katie. It had been six years. Could he trust her as he had before? Or had she lost that quality over the years?

"This was delightful, dear," Todd Logan said. "I'm ready for coffee."

"Oh, my, yes. Give me a minute." His mother gushed, wiped her mouth on her napkin, pushed her chair away from the table and stood. "Sorry. I'll get things ready and bring them right in."

"Can I help, Mrs. Logan—Lois?"

"No, no, my dear. You're our guest."

"Not a problem. It's what I do at Mariner's."

Mark took a deep breath as Katie followed his mother into the kitchen. He hadn't been able to take his eyes off her the entire time they were seated at the dining room table. His body, not to mention specific male parts, had been doing a dance the entire time. She was one sexy lady who didn't have a clue as to her beauty—her attraction. How in hell had he fallen out of love with her? Had he? The kiss they'd exchanged at her doorstep yesterday packed a powerful punch. The spark was still there. Had she felt it, too? Still, he needed to squelch those feelings. She was engaged.

His main objective was to provide a safe and consistent life for Kurtis. Registering him for daycare where his son could spend quality time with other children was important for Kurtis' social well-being. Leaving him with strangers was going to be difficult. Knowing Katie would be there would calm some of Kurtis' fears, as well as his own. Not that the kidnappers had a clue he'd returned to the States, or where to find him. But it never hurt to cover his tracks in order to protect his son.

Katelyn followed his mother from the kitchen, both carrying trays of coffee and dessert. Kurtis perked up when he saw the blueberry pie and ice cream.

"Ice cream," he shouted and clapped his hands.

"Do you want pie with that?" his mother asked.

"Ice cream," Kurtis repeated.

Katie scooped the vanilla ice cream while his mother cut the pie and put large pieces on their plates. The scent of wild blueberries bursting out of the crust circled the table, as did the aroma of freshly ground and brewed coffee. The room became quiet as everyone tucked into their dessert. Mark kept track of Katie from the corner of his eyes. She was nervous, her expression thoughtful. What was she thinking? If he had to guess, it was more than likely how to extricate herself from the situation she found herself in with his family. A family she hadn't had contact with in several years. He almost felt sorry for her being roped into having dinner with them. If he was honest, he was glad she hadn't backed down. And, as long as he was being honest with himself—he *had* missed her, more than he thought possible—just seeing her again…A sigh escaped. He couldn't get past the surge of warmth that filled his insides whenever she was near.

He'd lost track of the conversation and concentrated on his dessert. He hadn't had blueberry pie this good since he'd left Lobster Cove. Recognizing the sudden awkward silence, he searched for a safe topic.

"So, I was thinking of enrolling Kurtis at the daycare tomorrow. Will you be there?"

"I'm afraid not. I have my last exam of the semester. Linda Claussen will be there. She can help you. It's a perfect time to enroll Kurtis. We're planning a Christmas party soon. It will give him the opportunity to socially interact with the other children, and get to know them outside a more controlled atmosphere."

"How secure is the facility?"

"I'm not sure what you mean. I'm not aware of any problems."

"Son, I think someone is ready for his afternoon nap." His father nodded in Kurtis' direction.

Kurtis' head bobbed over his empty ice cream dish.

"I think you're right. If you'll excuse me, I'll only be a moment." Mark circled the table and lifted Kurtis from his chair and then carried him from the room. His son wasn't frail by any means, but the past few weeks had been life-changing, and no doubt tiring on his little body. It had been life-altering for him, as well. And even though he was up to the challenge of starting a new job—a new life—it didn't come without stress. Coming from a secure and loving family, Mark hadn't experienced the upheavals that his son was going through. He wanted that security and love for his son, as well. And it was up to him to provide it.

When he returned to the dining room, Katie stood next to the coffee table, her hands full of plates.

"Let me help you with the dishes before I leave," she offered.

"You will not lift a finger, young lady," his mother scolded. "Put those down. It was our pleasure to have your company today. Leave them. Todd will help me, won't you, dear?"

His father looked shell-shocked. Mark hid a smile. He couldn't remember a time when his father helped clear the table—apparently things hadn't changed in his absence if the comical look on his father's face was any indication.

"Go. You'll be busing a lot more dishes at Mariner's when you leave here."

"Thank you. Dinner was delicious. I enjoyed myself."

Mark followed her to the door and helped her on with her coat. She didn't look at him the entire time. Not able to resist, he spun her into his arms, put a finger under her chin, lifted her face up to meet his, and kissed her. He had only intended a light kiss goodbye, but once his lips met her tempting mouth, he was lost. He pressed his advantage and inserted his tongue in her mouth, pleased he hadn't met with the resistance he'd anticipated. Her arms raised, then froze in mid-air before they had a chance to wrap around his neck. Damn! He wasn't sorry about the kiss, only that she was having second thoughts—again—and rightfully so. She stepped away, leaving a gaping chasm between their overheated bodies.

"I'm not going to apologize, Katie. Seeing you again made me realize how much I've missed you."

"Don't, Mark. You've moved on. So have I. You can't keep kissing me like this. It's going to backfire, and I don't want anyone to get hurt."

"Have dinner with me one night this week. We can celebrate you finishing your exams."

"It's not a good idea. Really. You know I'm engaged."

"For old time's sake."

"What do you call this? We just had dinner with your parents."

"You know what I mean. This was uncomfortable as hell. We need to meet—alone. Talk without anyone else around. Will you at least think about it?"

He gazed into her eyes, quietly pleading with her to accept his invitation. He was an ass to force her hand, but there were things he wanted to tell her. Explain. Get off his chest. He wanted to know what she'd been doing the last six years besides going to college. Had she missed him?

"I'll think about it."

"Great. Good. I'll give you a call. How about tomorrow night? You can choose where you want to go."

"I can't tomorrow. I'll let you know. Goodbye, Mark."

Hell. He didn't want to let her go. He wanted to pull her in his arms, again, and kiss her senseless. Before he had a chance to claim those enticing lips, she opened the door and stepped outside into the sunny, but cold late afternoon air.

"I'll call Tuesday. We'll arrange something."

"We'll see."

She slipped inside her car and was down the road. He waved, but she didn't wave back. He ran his hand over his hair, his fingers meeting the short bristles of his military style haircut. He didn't know why watching Katie walk away made him feel as if he was losing her all over again.

But it did.

Shit. His world was spiraling out of control.

Chapter Six

She'd aced it! Katelyn walked out of the class room into the brisk winter air Monday morning and smiled. Her last exam for the semester was over. She could relax and enjoy Christmas and all the community festivities the town could throw her way. Looking forward to the kids' Christmas party and caroling at the town square gazebo, she started quietly singing "Sleigh Bells" as she walked across the crowded campus and headed toward her car.

"Hey, Katelyn, how'd your exam go?" Shelly from her psych class waved from across the quad.

Katelyn met her halfway. "A slam-dunk. How about you? What exam were you sitting for this morning?"

She'd met Shelly her first semester. They'd sat next to each other during orientation and had become college buddies ever since.

"Just turning in a paper. You and Sven set a date yet? I'm betting on a June wedding—right after graduation." Shelly hefted her backpack over her shoulder, and wrapped her purple and green scarf around her neck a bit tighter. A slight breeze carried a nip in the air, lifting her friend's short tresses around her face. Katelyn had tied her own long hair back, as usual, to keep it in place.

Shelly was in the midst of planning her own

nuptials, so the topic of her setting a date wasn't something she wanted to discuss at the moment. There was no date to reveal. She'd been trying to pin Sven down with a date for a whole year—to no avail. Seeing Shelly and knowing she was about to get married, made her anxious to set that date with Sven so she could visit Wedded Bliss and try on wedding gowns. The only reason she hadn't tried on gowns yet was not wanting to get ahead of herself and jinx the whole wedding planning thing. She was holding back, waiting for an official date to send out those "save the date" notices.

"Nope. No date yet," she admitted, tightening her own scarf. "Sven is in Norway visiting family. I'm sure when he returns we'll settle on something over Christmas break. But a June wedding would be lovely. Are you sticking around during winter break?"

"I'm going home. Ben and I have plans, mostly skiing. I'm about to head over to the snack bar before I head out. Want to join me?"

She didn't want to sit and discuss Shelly and Ben's romantic plans for winter break, and she certainly didn't want to listen to her classmate discuss their wedding plans. It was going to be a New Year's blowout. She and Sven were invited to attend. She hoped Sven would be back in plenty of time so she wouldn't have to go alone.

"Gosh, Shelly, I'd love to, but I promised my mom I'd stop in at Mariners before I went to the daycare for the afternoon. I'll catch up with you at the wedding. Tell Ben I said hi."

"It's a date. I'll see you in January at our wedding. Isn't it exciting? I can hardly wait."

Shelly gave her a hug, waved goodbye, and set off

back across campus. Katelyn tightened her own scarf against the cold as she scurried down the sidewalk toward her car. Her thoughts about the wedding and no date swirled around in her mind.

She made a quick stop at Mariners for a lobster roll and cola, and then headed over to Hearts and Hands. The minute she walked in the room, Kurtis spotted her and attacked her legs.

"Katie!" His excitement was bittersweet. She was growing much too fond of Mark's son already. She had to guard her heart—and his.

"Hi, Kurtis." She patted his head, his hair fine and flighty, then leaned over and gave him a brief hug. "I'm glad you're here. Have you met the other children?"

"I made sure he did." Linda joined them, putting her hand on Kurtis' shoulder. "He's a bit shy—not unusual for the first day, and having to meet so many new faces."

"I'm sure he'll join in with the others by the end of the week. He's a very personable boy."

As if to prove her right, Kurtis cut loose and ran to where Connie Blye's son, Jason, was constructing a tall structure in the building block corner.

"He and Jason hit it off right away," Linda said. "Unusual for Jason. It could be just what the two of them need."

"That would be a good thing."

Connie Blye had been two or three years behind her in high school—she didn't know her very well. But Linda had mentioned that Connie had married Jason Blye right out of high school. After their son Jason was born, Connie's husband died of an incurable cancer. Jason was a quiet, reserved child, but it was obvious

Connie loved her son and was doing the best she could to raise him on her own. It was good to see Jason and Kurtis hitting it off so fast.

"I've got to say, Mark was full of questions about the security at Hearts and Hands when he dropped Kurtis off this morning." Linda locked the door and made sure the "ring the bell" sign was in place. "He wanted to make sure the doors were locked during session, and that the kids were thoroughly chaperoned at all times. He even wanted to know what the ratio of kids was to adults. I told him we followed state regulations to a T. Is something wrong? Something we should know about?"

Katelyn blinked, mentally shook her head, and forced herself to recall if Mark had said anything about a potential problem. The only thing she remembered was his concern about finding a "safe" home for his son, and the question concerning the safety of the day care. She'd considered Mark was only being a thoughtful and caring father. Was there something else going on that she wasn't aware of? Had she missed the obvious? Mr. and Mrs. Logan hadn't acted as if there was anything afoul.

Linda was putting doubts in her head—conjuring trouble where there was none.

"You do know his line of work in the military was top secret, right? I'm sure security has been ingrained in him over the years, and hard to let go of on a personal level. His wife died and Kurtis is without a mother, so I'm not surprised Mark is doubly cautious about his care."

"Oh. I didn't know his wife had died. It must be hard on the both of them."

"I'm sure it's nothing to worry about, otherwise he surely would have said something."

"You're probably right. So how did your last exam go?" Linda scanned the room, making sure everything was in order, all the children were busy and not misbehaving before she turned back to Katelyn, eyebrows raised in question.

"I aced it. Glad the semester is over. I'll be able to spend more time at the daycare if you need me."

"You bet. In fact, you can start in the kitchen—lunch is over and the kitchen needs cleaning."

"Bad timing on my part." Katelyn laughed. "Seriously, I don't mind. What do you have planned for story hour?" She followed Linda through the maze of play stations, and around the indoor raised sandbox where Celia and Randy were sifting sand in measuring cups and redistributing it in the corners.

"The chart says it's Sandy and Trish's turn to pick out a book. You'll have to ask them. They've been at the bookstand in the corner nook all morning trying to decide."

The rest of the afternoon flew by, leaving little time for her and Linda to go over the plans for the Christmas party on Friday. Without warning, Mark was there to pick up Kurtis. Katelyn's insides gave a jolt when she looked straight into his sparkling eyes, so like Kurtis'. His smile had her smiling back, even though she was nervously biting the inside of her cheek, remembering his kisses.

He knelt, pulled Kurtis into his big arms, and hugged his son. All Katelyn could think of was yesterday when he'd walked her to the door after dinner. He'd held her hand, swung her around, pulled her into those strong, firm arms, and kissed her—another one of his toe-curling, knee-bending, heart-stopping kisses that brought memories flooding to her lower regions. She'd wanted to melt into his arms, but had come to her senses and held back. The whole day had been surreal—just like old times, except this time she wasn't dating the Logans' son. She was engaged to Sven, and the reality had hit her like a bucket of ice, once again. The minute she left the Logans' house, she got in her car, and buckled the seatbelt—the click of metal clasping metal bringing her back to her senses. It had been foolish to accept their dinner invitation and think it wouldn't bring back memories better left buried.

And like the click of the seatbelt, Connie Blye entered the center, bumping into Mark and the two of them were in each other's arms—hugging. Katelyn helped Celia with the buttons on her coat, all the while watching Mark from the corner of her eyes as he wrapped his arms around Connie. Connie's hug appeared a bit tighter than a mere friendly hug. The two stared at each other for a moment, as if they were contemplating kissing, and instead, stepped out of each other's arms. Katelyn could only covertly stare at the two of them. She'd never seen Connie so animated—all smiles.

Connie was a beautiful woman, not tall and gangly like she was, but the woman had a presence about her that was endearing. Her short, sable hair was well taken care of, and her clothes, although not the latest styles, were always neat and did her full-bodied stature justice. She wasn't aware Mark knew Connie. Apparently, there was a lot about Mark she didn't know.

Jason joined Kurtis, and the four of them talked and laughed together. The warmth flowing from them spoke volumes—they resembled a loving family. Taking a deep breath and shaking her head, she was about to turn away when Mark's piercing blue eyes looked at her as if he might come her way. His attention, however, was distracted. Katelyn made her escape, but not before she overheard them discussing a play date for the boys before she made it to the coat closet to get coats for several of the other children. She scolded herself for eavesdropping, and for getting… what? Jealous? No! She wasn't jealous. Why should she be jealous? She was happy Mark and Kurtis had found someone to connect with. Mark and Connie had both lost their spouses. Their sons had each lost a parent. They had a lot in common, and it was only natural for them to be drawn together.

After the last child was picked up, Linda plunked down in the nearest child size chair. "Whew! What a day. Got a minute so we can go over the plans for Friday's party?"

Katelyn pulled a chair out from under the table and joined her.

"Not really. I'm expected at Mariner's tonight, and I want to get home and change. Get my comfy shoes on. Besides, my mind is fried right now. How about we come in a half hour earlier in the morning before everyone arrives?"

"That would work. I am tired. Let's close up and go home."

Katelyn hoped keeping occupied at the restaurant would help get her mind off Mark and Connie.

And Sven's absence.

Katelyn was in the process of preparing to jump in the shower when the phone rang. She wrapped a towel around her naked body, padded barefoot across the floor, and lifted the receiver.

"Hello, Katelyn. Glad I caught you at home."

"Sven! I miss you," she gushed. "I'm so glad you called. How was the anniversary celebration?" She sat on the edge of the bed and crossed her legs.

"The celebration was a success, but short lived. *Bestefar* was taken ill, and had to be rushed to the hospital. Turns out he's developed pneumonia. They want to monitor him for a few days, especially after the mini-stroke."

"I assume *Bestefar* is your grandfather?"

"Sorry, yes. I tend to revert to Norwegian when I'm here. My *Bestemor*—sorry, my grandmother—didn't take it well."

"Oh, Sven. I'm so sorry. I hope they both mend quickly. I'm sure they're pleased you and your parents are there to help."

"The doctors say they have every reason to believe he'll recover. He's a strong Norseman for sure."

"I'm sorry to hear he's in the hospital, but glad he'll recover. Does this mean you'll be flying home sooner than planned?"

There was a silent pause while Katelyn waited for his answer. She pressed the phone closer to her ear and shut her eyes, not wanting to miss his reply.

"Sven? Can you hear me? Are you still there?"

"Yes, sorry. I was trying to decide whether I should share the family news before my parents pass the word around back home. I trust you to keep it to yourself and not spread the word until my parents have a chance to break the news."

Another pause had her breath catching and her heart beating double time. What was Sven trying to say? Would he not be home for Christmas after all? Disappointment settled at the bottom of her stomach.

"Sven?"

"My parents are selling Flowers in Bloom. They are going to return to Bergen, permanently, to take care of *Bestefar* and *Bestemor.*" Another long pause. "And to run the family business here. My father met with the lawyer in Bergen and signed all the papers this morning. It's a done deal. My grandfather's fishing business has officially been transferred to my father."

This time it was Katelyn who remained silent, trying to catch her breath. Oh my God! What did this mean? Was Sven out of a job?

She swallowed, and closed her eyes. "What are you going to do, Sven? Are you going to take over Flowers in Bloom?" She held her breath, waiting for his answer.

The prolonged silence on the other end of the line had her bouncing one leg over the other in nervous anticipation. He sounded so cautious, so distant. What was Sven not telling her?

Her throat dried up, she couldn't swallow. She slid off the bed onto the floor, the phone clutched in a tight fist against her ear, her other hand gripped the end of her shirttail. Sven had anticipated taking over the business someday. He'd spent every waking moment he hadn't spent with her catering to and for the business. The family was an integral part of the community—and well liked. She couldn't imagine Lobster Cove without Jance and Inge Olson. Or Flowers in Bloom.

"Sven?"

"No. I'm not really sure where that leaves me. I'll have to look for another job, or see if I can work for the new owners. I haven't made up my mind yet."

"What? Oh, Sven. I'm so sorry. What will you do?" She stood and paced around the room in circles.

"We'll discuss it when I come back to Lobster Cove. The parents have already gotten the ball rolling on the business end back there."

"When are you coming home?"

"Things are complicated right now. I'll let you know. I can't leave my parents to deal with this alone. They need my help and support over the holidays, not to mention helping to take care of the grandparents."

"I understand. But I'll miss you. Do you think you'll make it home for Christmas?"

"I've got to go. I'll call in a couple days and let you know how things are going."

"I love you. Give your parents my love."

The phone disconnected on the other end of the line. Katelyn held the receiver at arm's length and looked at it as if it would offer an excuse for the abrupt closure. When no explanation was forthcoming, she placed the phone back on the side table, walked to the window, and stared out at the large snowflakes falling lazily toward the frozen ground.

Was it snowing in Bergen? Was the town decorated for Christmas? Sven hadn't said. Actually, he hadn't said much of anything. His usual effervescent voice sounded flat, hesitant, and…tired? Of course, he was worried about his grandparents, and the fact he might not have a job when he returned to Lobster Cove. Understandable, really. Darn it. She couldn't wait for

Sven to fly back home so he could fill her in on everything. Witnessing her best friend Juelle's family problems taught her how all-consuming it could be on everyone. She wished she was in Bergen so she could help Sven and his parents get through this difficult time.

Katelyn showered, dried off, and quickly dressed in a pair of black slacks and a red turtleneck sweater. She pulled her hair back in a long ponytail and grabbed her coat and car keys. She shut the fire down in the fireplace, and slid the glass door shut in front of the dying embers, then unplugged the tree lights. She had just enough time to make it to Mariner's and beat the evening crowd in time to help her parents.

As usual, Mariner's was hopping. Her mother greeted her with a worried frown and nodded her head toward the kitchen.

"What's wrong?" Katelyn looked toward the kitchen as she unbuttoned her coat and headed toward the employee's lounge.

"Claude had to take his son to the emergency room. He fell on the ice, skating. They think he's broken his arm. Michael O'Toole is trying to take over the kitchen in his absence, but he hasn't the experience and is falling behind. Even your father is having a hard time keeping things moving tonight."

"What gives? It's Monday. Usually a slower night now that the summer crowd is gone."

"Must be the holiday season."

"Or your holiday special."

"Remind me not to offer blueberry cobbler on a Monday night again. In any case, glad you're here. Can you take this order over to table twenty-three for me? I'll head back to the kitchen and see if I can give

Michael a hand."

Katelyn delivered the main course to table twenty-three. When she turned around, she spotted Mark sitting at a booth in the far corner with Chief of Police, Daryl Johnson. The two were in deep discussion, both leaning over the top of the table, foreheads nearly touching, as if not wanting anyone in close proximity to hear what they were discussing. Deciding not to interrupt, she left them to it and headed back to the kitchen. Was Linda right? Was there a problem? Was Mark overly concerned with Kurtis' safety that he had to talk to the police? Linda's concern suddenly took on more serious implications.

"Katelyn, honey, can you get me some of your mother's blueberry cobbler." Henry Bilson flagged her down as she was passing by.

"Sure thing, Henry. You two want ice cream with that?" He and his wife were regulars whenever they made it down from Ellsworth—a friendly, older couple that were such sweethearts.

"Course, darling, Ramona and I each want two scoops."

"How's that beau of yours?" Mrs. Bilson asked, a dimple in her plump cheek and a twinkle in her eyes.

"He's in Norway celebrating his grandparents' fiftieth wedding anniversary."

"Oh, how wonderful. We celebrated our fiftieth two years ago, didn't we, Henry?"

Henry shook his head in agreement, and gazed adoringly into his wife's eyes. "Yep. Fifty-two years."

Katelyn sighed. Would she and Sven make it to fifty years? She couldn't comprehend being married to him—or anyone for that matter—for that length of time.

"I'll be right back with your dessert."

Katelyn gave Michael O'Toole the orders.

"Be sure to put two scoops of vanilla ice cream on these. I'll be back in a sec."

Michael took the piece of paper she'd handed him, shook his head and proceeded to fill the order. Katelyn tucked her arm around the serving tray and turned, only to bump into her mother.

"Careful, dear. Don't want to dump my entire tray of dirty dishes."

"Sorry, didn't see you come up behind me."

"I've got it under control."

"Did you know Mark was here with Chief Johnson?"

"Yes, over in the corner booth."

"Is everything okay?" She recalled her conversation with Linda about security.

"I don't know. Tess Highland called and said something about Homeland Security and confidentiality when she made the reservation for the Chief. Something about Homeland Security working with the police and the National Guard along the coast and Canadian border. I made sure they had a private table in the back."

"You think Mark is working for the Department of Homeland Security? He didn't mention it at dinner yesterday." The topic had been brushed aside during dinner at his parent's home. In fact, she had no idea what type of job he was looking for, now that he was back in Lobster Cove. Maybe her mother was right. Maybe he was talking to Chief Johnson about a job.

"Makes you wonder what he really did in the

military, doesn't it?"

"Hmmm. I think there's a lot we don't know about Mark. His family has been very quiet about his absence in Lobster Cove."

"Maybe now that he's back we'll find out."

"Maybe." Only time would tell.

"So, has my future son-in-law called? Thought he'd be back home by now."

"Sven called as soon as I got home from daycare this afternoon. Apparently, things have become a bit complicated in Norway." She had promised not to tell anyone about the Olson's selling Flowers in Bloom, and that included her mother. Keeping it to herself, and the fact Sven hadn't sounded like himself over the phone, didn't sit well. She'd always confided in her mother and was ill at ease keeping this bit of news to herself.

"His grandfather is in the hospital and his grandmother is having a hard time dealing with everything. The Olsons are staying in Bergen a bit longer than planned to make sure everything goes well. Sven wasn't sure when he'd be back."

"I'm sorry, honey. I know how much you love Christmas, and not having Sven around to help celebrate it with you has got to be hard. But don't let that stop you from enjoying the holiday."

"I'm trying not to. I am looking forward to the kids' Christmas party on Friday. In fact, Linda and I are going to put the finishing touches on it tomorrow morning. Carolyn Clark said she'd be there to help—she doesn't want to miss out on the party, either."

"I'm glad she can make it. Carolyn is such lovely woman. I understand she's great with the kids. So, how was dinner at the Logans'?"

Michael rang the bell behind them, ending their discussion just in time. She didn't want to discuss Mark with her mother right now. Seeing him hugging Connie was unsettling—especially after she'd been in his arms and on the receiving end of one of his sexy kisses the day before.

"We're right here, Michael." Dawn Sullivan scowled. "No need to ring that dang thing so loud when we're standing right next to you."

Michael's face turned beet red from embarrassment as he slide two dishes of cobbler with ice cream toward Katelyn, and a tray full of steaming lobster and all the fixings toward her mother.

"If it remains this hectic," her mother said over her shoulder, "I'm going to advertise for a part-time waitress for the holiday. Not to mention another chef, depending on how long Claude will be away. You know his wife Martha can't cope with this right now; she's recently had a knee replacement."

"Maybe a high school senior would like to earn some extra cash this time of year."

"Smart idea. I'll get right on that. You'd better get the cobbler served before the ice cream melts."

Chapter Seven

Katelyn was late arriving at daycare Tuesday morning and had to ring the bell to be let in.

"I'm so sorry, Linda. You're probably ready to fire me. I was so exhausted when I left Mariner's last night, I crashed and forgot to set the alarm." Katelyn couldn't remember when she'd ever forgotten to set the alarm. Perplexed over Sven's confusing phone call, worried he wouldn't make it home for Christmas, seeing Mark with Chief Johnson, not to mention the cozy scene with Connie Blye yesterday, and why that should bother her, she'd simply kicked off her shoes and flopped into bed.

"You aren't fired. I didn't get here early, either. Stayed up too late last night planning our Christmas dinner with my girls."

"Whew, that makes me feel better. So, what do you want me to do for the party? I have plenty of time to help now that classes are over. What's on the agenda for today?"

"With so many younger children enrolled this fall, we need to keep it simple. I talked to some of the parents this morning, and they've agreed to provide cookies and drinks. I don't think we need much more than that, do you?

"You're right. The kids will be so ramped up with excitement as it is, extra sugar will just put them over the top. But that reminds me, my mother is making cut out sugar cookies tonight so the kids can decorate them tomorrow. I'll stop by the grocery mart before I go to the restaurant and see if Helen has some neat decorating toppings."

"Now all we need is a Santa to distribute the gifts."

"Ask Mark. He was the one who played Santa at the lodge."

"What? Really? How'd you find out?"

"He actually confessed."

"Think you could ask him if he'd be interested? The kids would love it."

"We can check when he comes to get Kurtis this afternoon." She really didn't want to be the one to ask, and remind him he'd seen her in that horrid elf outfit, regardless of how sexy he thought she looked in it. But this was for the kids, so she'd give in and thrust her pride aside and ask. "What about gifts for Santa to hand out? What did you have in mind?"

"Got that covered. Jan Williams said we could pick out an appropriate toy for each child from the Church of God's Toys for Tots campaign. Apparently they've been so successful this year they have an overabundance. I invited her and our director, Jolene, to come to the party, too."

"Wonderful. I overheard Noelia Russo tell Helen Troy that St. Joseph's Ladies of the Rosary Society's annual coat drive was doing extremely well, too. I'm sure we have a few kids who could use a warm coat this winter. I can ask and see if they'd be willing to help out."

"Definitely. I'll make a list of gender and sizes. Hopefully, they can find one for each of our kids—it will make a nice additional present."

"If not, I know for a fact Eugenia McClintock still manages several funds through McClintock and McClintock and is very generous this time of year. I understand she makes sure the food pantry is well stocked, too."

"I just love it when the town comes together this time of year."

"I can't imagine living anywhere else." Except Norway, and only long enough to help Sven during his family's crisis. If he couldn't be home for Christmas, she would go to him. If she left Friday, right after the children's party, she'd be there Saturday, mid-morning. Yes! The more she thought about it the better the idea sounded. She would check on flights as soon as she got home tonight and see if she could make arrangements.

"Reminds me, did you know Eugenia's house is on the market?"

"Yes, Mark mentioned he was going to be looking for a home—his mother mentioned it. But he's not interested in the McClintock estate. Said it's too large."

"Rumor has it Eugenia and Günter Jordan have been off traveling the last few months. Not sure what's going on between them, but as usual, the rumor mill is active."

"It's a shame what she experienced last year. Losing her husband to a heart attack, then her son in a freak accident in a storm. Still, it was nothing compared to what she and her son put Juelle through."

"So glad it all worked out for Juelle. Are Juelle and her new husband still in control of McClintock and McClintock Lobster Company?"

"As far as I know. They bought a house here, so I'm assuming they're still involved. I haven't talked to

Juelle lately. But she so deserves happiness after finding out her first husband had cheated on her before his death."

"Oh, right. I forget. It was with Nora Spears, right?"

Katelyn hadn't seen Nora since the episode at Sebastian's funeral when she fell apart over his death. Juelle had been shocked to discover the two of them had been having an affair and practically cleaned out his bank account. She should call Juelle and wish her a Merry Christmas and see how things were going in Hawaii.

By the time lunch rolled around, Katelyn's mind was abuzz with thoughts of flying across the Atlantic to Norway to be with Sven. Just thinking about going to Norway had her unable to concentrate on anything else. What fun, to jump a plane and surprise her fiancé. If she left this Friday, she would have plenty of time to spend with Sven and his family, and still be home in time to spend Christmas with her own family. And who knew, maybe he would fly back home with her.

Once the children were settled quietly for an after-lunch rest period, Katelyn took Linda aside. Seated across the round kitchen table from each other, drinking a steaming hot cup of tea, she filled her friend in on her idea.

"I'm thinking of booking a flight to join Sven in Norway. His grandfather is doing poorly, so he isn't able to come home for Christmas. He sounded down in the dumps when he called last night. I feel as if I should be there to help. Lend him moral support. Surprise him. What do you think?"

"Oh, Katelyn, what a fantastic idea. When were

you planning on going?"

"I thought this Friday, right after the Christmas party. That is, if I can get a flight."

"Call the airlines right now. Set it up. Why wait?"

"I don't know. I don't want his family to think I'm imposing, but I have a strong urge to be there for him. Ease his worry."

"I think it's a wonderful idea. Really, Katelyn, don't hesitate. We'll be finished here on Friday until after the holidays, anyway. It'll be a great little getaway. I'm sure Sven would love it if you surprised him. What a romantic Christmas present."

"I'll have to talk to my parents. Make sure they can get along without my help for a few days. I know my mother was going to hire extra help. I'll talk to her tonight and see what she thinks."

"Don't wait too long to make reservations. It might be difficult this time of year."

"I won't. Thanks for the moral support."

They finished their tea. Katelyn rinsed her cup, and put it in the drainer. "Come on, we'd better get today's craft project prepared before we have a handful of bored kids on our hand this afternoon."

The rest of the afternoon was busy with the children working on projects. By the time parents started arriving to take their children home, she was more than ready to call it a day. Katelyn kept an eye out for Mark, who was the last to arrive. Kurtis was waiting in the library area, looking at a book about dogs.

It was now or never. She took a deep breath, let it out, and approached him. He smiled, causing her to trip over her own feet.

"Hi, Mark, I wanted to catch you before Kurtis

spots you. As you know, we're having a Christmas party on Friday for the kids and their parents."

"Great. Can I do anything to help?"

Katelyn couldn't believe he'd given her the perfect opening. She bit the inside of her cheek and lowered her eyes, then looked back into those sexy eyes of his, and that killer dimple.

"Umm, well, Linda was wondering if you would play Santa for the children. It would only be for a short time. You did such a wonderful job at Breakfast with Santa. The kids loved you. Many of the kids from here attended, and it would be great if they were to see the same Santa. It would reinforce their belief, and be less confusing."

He didn't hesitate.

"On one condition. You be my elf and help me hand out the gifts."

"What! No. No way!"

"It's the only way I'll do it. Take it or leave it."

"We have enough little elves running around. You don't really expect me to wear that silly outfit again?"

"Sure I do. You looked great in it and the kids loved it."

"Why are you doing this?"

"Let's just say, together we make a great team. Come on, Katie. It'll be fun working together again."

"This is blackmail."

"So, you'll do it?"

"Do I have a choice?"

"Nope."

"I'll think about it."

"Daddy!" Kurtis ran toward his father and crashed into his legs.

"Hi, bud. Get your coat so we can take off. Grandma is waiting dinner for us."

"Want dog."

"We'll talk about a dog later."

"Puppy." Kurtis showed him the book he'd been reading. The cover had an adorable black lab puppy with a red collar. Kurtis pointed at the picture.

"Give Katie the book, bud." He turned to her, "We'll talk about this later."

Reluctantly, Kurtis handed her the book.

"Thanks." Katelyn tucked the book under her arm.

"Have dinner with me tonight?" Mark asked.

His words startled her. What was he up to? She'd told him she was engaged.

"I have to work at the restaurant tonight. Perhaps another time." She wasn't about to spend time alone with Mark. Having Sunday dinner at his parents' was one thing. Just the two of them? It wasn't going to happen. Being alone with him wasn't going to help her keep her resolve one bit. There was no sense rekindling old feelings, when both of them knew it was going nowhere.

"You know I'm engaged, right?"

"So you said. I haven't seen this fiancé of yours— if he is real."

"He's real." Maybe if she told him she was planning to join Sven in Norway he'd believe her and back off.

"Daddy!" Kurtis fidgeted trying to get his arms into his winter coat.

"Come here, bud. Let me help you with your coat." Mark finished buttoning Kurtis into his outerwear, then lifted him in his strong arms. "Tell Katie goodbye."

102

"Bye, Katie."

"Bye, Kurtis."

"I'll see you later. I'll call so we can set something up." His smile said he wasn't taking no for an answer.

Katelyn closed the door behind him, and turned to finish helping Linda.

"So? Did you ask him? What'd he say?"

She didn't want to tell Linda she'd been blackmailed into playing elf to his Santa. She shook her head and sighed.

"Uh-oh. From that heavy sigh I have a feeling things didn't go as smooth as we contemplated."

Linda might have contemplated things going without a hitch, but she hadn't.

"He had stipulations—wants me to play his elf."

"Fantastic. The kids will love it. Why didn't I think of that to begin with? We can all wear elf hats, too. In fact, it will be our theme for the afternoon. The kids can make elf hats out of green and red construction paper, tomorrow."

"You dress up in a similar outfit on Friday and I'll be happier. You have no idea how ridiculous I felt. I still haven't forgiven my father.

Would she ever live the elf incident down? It was the last time she'd let her father talk her into putting on such a display. She was getting too old and was too tall to parade around in a bright and cheesy elf outfit.

"I'm sure your father isn't worried. He knows you'll get over it."

By the time Katelyn stopped at the grocery mart and picked out chocolate chips, a small box of raisins, red, blue, yellow and green icing tubes, various colored sugar sprinkles, and powdered sugar, she had just enough time to stop and fill the car up with gas before she was due at Mariner's. Her mother waved as she made a mad dash for the employee's lounge. Katelyn waved back.

"I'll be with you in a sec, Mom."

"Under control. Take your time."

Katelyn glanced around the festive dining room all aglow with flickering lights, garland, red bells hanging all around the room, and candles burning behind tall glass globes in the middle of each table. But her mother was right—they weren't very busy, yet—only half the tables were occupied. She checked her watch. It was only six-thirty. Things were bound to pick up, depending on what else was going on in the neighborhood. She made her way to the lounge, put her coat and purse in a locker, kicked off her boots, and slipped into her work shoes. She ran a comb through her hair, pulled it back into a braid this time, and then put on a bright red lobster Christmas apron with the restaurant's logo on the front. She joined her mother in the dining area.

"I hired two seniors from the high school for the holiday. One of them started tonight. Thankfully, it's slow so she'll have an easy time of it."

"Who did you hire?"

"Aimee Hart and Kimberly Ashford. Aimee has taken over like she was born to be a waitress—a great personality, too. Kimberly starts Friday. Let's hope she's a good fit for our crowd."

"Great. Maybe we can keep them during the summer, too."

"I'll talk to your father, and see what he thinks."

"Before we get too busy, Mom, I need to talk to

you about something. I'm thinking about going to Norway to be with Sven. Linda thinks it's a great idea, but I'm not so sure."

"Is something wrong, dear? What's going on?"

"Other than his grandfather's mini-stroke, he's in the hospital with pneumonia. His grandmother is having a hard time coping. I'm sure everything else is going to be fine. I guess I'm just feeling a bit lonely this time of year, myself." She couldn't tell her mother about Sven's parents moving back to Bergen and selling the business here in Lobster Cove. "Besides, I think he could use my support, especially this time of year. He sounded kind of depressed."

"My dear, if you feel that strongly about going, you should go. Of course you should. I'm sure Sven and his family will appreciate your concern and willingness to be of help."

"I don't know how long I'll be gone. I want to be home with you and Dad for Christmas."

"Now, don't you worry about us. You stay with Sven and help him and his family through their crisis. But what about getting a flight this time of year? It might be difficult. When were you planning to leave?"

"I was thinking about leaving Friday night, after the daycare's Christmas party. I wanted to talk to you first before I check on arrangements. I'm hoping I can catch a flight."

"You let me take care of making the arrangements. It'll be your father's and my Christmas present to you and Sven." She pulled Katelyn into her arms. "You are such a lovely daughter, you deserve to go and enjoy. Please don't worry about a thing, here. You go and stay as long as you need to—as long as Sven and his family need you. They are so lucky that you will soon be part of their family."

"Thanks, Mom." Katelyn hugged her mother, kissed her cheek, and sighed. Her stomach bunched. She hoped she was doing the right thing. She grabbed an order pad and pencil and turned to face the room. And froze. Mark had just stepped inside, and was heading her way.

"Hey, Katie. I thought if you didn't have time to have dinner with me, I'd come by and have dinner here—with you."

"Sorry, I just arrived. I don't have time."

"It doesn't look very busy to me. I'll just sit over at that booth until you catch a break."

"Where's Kurtis?"

"Mom and Dad are watching him—wanted some 'quality' time with their grandson."

"Why are you doing this, Mark?"

His smile was disarming. She shouldn't let him get to her like this.

"For old times' sake, Katie. Just a bit of catching up—see what you've been doing all these years. Talk between old friends?"

"I had dinner at your parent's Sunday. Remember? We talked then." Not to mention kissed!

"But *we* didn't have a chance to *talk*."

"Hey, Katelyn, you gonna take our order or what?" Saved by a customer.

"Gotta go. Sorry."

"I'll be right over here. Waiting."

Business picked up considerably, and the evening disappeared. One minute Mark was eating, the next, the booth he was sitting in was empty. She didn't have a chance to sit and talk, and had mixed emotions over him leaving before she'd had a chance to see what he really wanted. Confused over his departure without saying he was leaving, she met her mother at the checkout booth.

"Great news. I managed to get you a flight, but it's not direct, and it's not first-class seating. It goes to Amsterdam, first, and then on to Bergen. You do have a passport, right? I forgot to ask if you had one. I'm not sure you can get one in time, if you don't."

"I have one, Mom. When Sven made our engagement official, I thought I might have an opportunity to go to Norway someday. I wanted to be prepared."

"Problem solved. Go home and get some rest. Oh. Wait. Here are the cookies for the kids to decorate tomorrow. Have fun." Her mother handed her a covered baking sheet piled high with cut out sugar cookies. "There are a few gingerbread, too."

"Wow. When did you find time to bake all these?"

"I had Michael O'Toole bake them for me. Turns out he's a great pastry chef."

"Thank him for me. The kids will have a ball with these tomorrow."

"Wish I could be there to help. Enjoy."

Katelyn placed the cookies on the floor in the back seat of her car so they wouldn't slide out and crumble. She took her time driving home, and carefully pulled into her driveway, only to step on the brakes.

Mark's car sat idling in front of the house.

Chapter Eight

What was Mark doing parked in front of her house at this hour? What was so important he had to sit in his car waiting for her to get home this late at night? He stepped out of his car, palmed the lock fob, and walked toward her. Not meeting his eyes, easy to do in the dark, she got out of her own vehicle, opened the back door, and lifted the tray of cookies from the floor. Thankfully, they hadn't slid around when she slammed on the breaks. They were all intact. She shut the door with her fanny, turned around, and faced him.

"What are you doing here?"

"I need to talk to you. May I come in?"

"Sorry, we were busy tonight. I didn't get a chance to take a break and join you before you left. When I finally had a break, you were gone."

"No problem. I won't stay long. Here, let me take those for you. Christmas cookies? They smell delicious."

"Yes. They're for the kids to decorate tomorrow at daycare." Katelyn handed him the tray, and walked to the porch, digging in her coat pocket to retrieve the house key.

"I can't imagine having the patience to deal with a handful of kids in the presence of icing and cookies."

"It does get messy. But it's a lot of fun."

Once inside, Katelyn invited Mark to take his coat

off and have a seat while she took the cookies to the kitchen. When she returned, he had the tree lights plugged in, and a fire going in the grate—a soft glow filled the room. Almost romantic. Almost. But Katelyn wasn't quite feeling it. Mark's demeanor was anything but romantic, and that was a good thing. Wasn't it? Whatever he wanted to talk to her about had to be important if it couldn't wait until tomorrow—or the next day. She sat on one end of the sofa and waited for him to have a seat. He didn't. Instead, he started pacing. Uh oh, this didn't look good.

"I owe you an apology," he blurted, his hands sliding into his slacks' pockets. "I need to explain about the last six years—clear the air between us."

"You don't need to explain anything, Mark. It's all in the past where it belongs. We're both in different places now."

Should she tell him about her pregnancy? Her miscarriage? But to what end? It had no bearing on the present—on their lives, their separate futures.

"Please, Katie, just hear me out. Although there are things I can't talk about, I want you to know I only ever had your best interest at heart when I didn't keep in touch with you. Or anyone back home for that matter. It was too dangerous. Our missions were top secret—and hazardous. To the point that anyone connected with us could be in danger."

It explained a lot, but mostly what she had already presumed. She waited while he paced, then stood in front of the tree for a moment, his back to her. He turned, approached the sofa, and stood looking down at her. It made her feel small and alone sitting by herself, his height towering overhead. She crossed her arms and waited for him to continue. She could see the indecision in his eyes, his face, and his stance. This wasn't easy for him. But then, she wasn't feeling very easy about Mark's return to Lobster Cove or him standing in front of her, trying to put his own feeling to rest, either.

"I was given a complete alternate identity—looks, background, you name it—it wasn't me. Even you, or my parents, wouldn't have recognized me. I can't go into any more detail about that part of my life, only to say it was for the best."

"In case you have to use that disguise again?" It made sense, which meant he wasn't going to be in Lobster Cove long after all.

"Yes. Contact with anyone back home could have put their lives in jeopardy, as well as the operations. You meant too much to me, Katie. I couldn't let something happen to you—to my parents. I could never live with myself if that happened."

She understood, but his defection—walking away from what they had shared, had the old hurt erupting to the surface. Keeping it in was driving her crazy. She jumped from the couch, almost knocking into him. He stepped back, his brows raised in surprise.

"I waited two years for word from you before I gave up, Mark. Two years! Do you know how your lack of communication made me feel inside? I felt abandoned. I thought we had something special. I loved you!"

In seconds she was pulled into his arms in a tight embrace, her head against his chest. She couldn't help but snuggle into his enticing body. She drank in his male scent, his fragrant cologne. Listening to his beating heart filled her senses. It was like being held in his arms six years ago—as if he'd never left her. She was drunk on his essence. Her head spun, and she slid her arms around his neck, stood on tiptoes, and leaned into his devouring kiss—a kiss that had her heart soaring. His arms tugged her closer, his lips prying hers apart. His tongue begging entrance, she opened greedily. His strong hands bunched her sweater mere seconds before she felt the firm pressure of those fingers unfasten her bra. Her breasts released, caught in his cupped capable hands. Her knees folded. She leaned against him. He lowered her to the floor, never letting go. Wrapped in his embrace, the kiss continued. Katelyn swore she'd died and gone to heaven. His mouth left hers only to splay many tiny ardent kisses along her neck, her shoulder, then lower.

"Oh, Katie," he murmured. "I was hoping you felt the same. Seeing you in that sexy elf outfit after all these years…God. My heart about jumped out of my chest."

Katelyn froze. What the hell was she doing? Did he think because they once had a thing for each other she'd be willing to have sex with him because he thought she a made a "sexy elf"? He knew she was engaged. What kind of person did he think she was if she was willing to have sex with him while engaged to someone else? Oh, my God! What kind of person was she? She'd almost cheated on Sven!

"Stop. Mark. I can't do this."

"God, Katie, I've missed you. We're made for each other."

"But you married someone else!" she shouted. "You had a child with someone else." Katelyn pushed him aside, pulled her sweater down over her aching breasts, away from his seductive, charismatic charms. She didn't care if his face was full of pain—regret. That he might be hurting, too. He had no idea what she'd gone through—what she'd lost. She had to tell him.

"If it's any consolation, I only married Natasha because she was pregnant—it was the right thing to do at the time."

She turned her back on him and walked to the window. Did she really want to hear this? Just because he needed to get it off his chest? She wasn't ready to listen—to hear about his love affair with another woman.

"Please. Just go, Mark. You don't need to fill in the blanks." She cringed, shut her eyes as he ignored her plea and continued.

"Natasha and I were paired together as a married couple for the last three assignments. We spent so much time together on those ops, we became fond of each other. Much of our time together was spent in hotel rooms, attending political events where we had to make it look as if our marriage was real. Our rooms were bugged, so we had to act the part, and well, I guess we got carried away one night."

"Mark—"

"No, let me finish. I'm so sorry, Katie. When Kurtis was born, I wanted to make sure he had my name—make it official, make sure he was safe. So we married. But our life-style wasn't conducive to family life—not like back home here in Lobster Cove. As soon as Natasha was able, she jumped at the chance to go back to work. In any case, she wasn't thrilled at being a mother. She signed on for one more mission. I tried to talk her out of it, for Kurtis' sake, but she was adamant and refused. Unfortunately, things didn't go as planned. I can't discuss the particulars, only to say that the op was a setup. The entire team was ambushed. Natasha was killed, along with several others."

"I'm sorry, Mark. It must have been awful for you. And for Kurtis." She couldn't imagine the hell he'd gone through living like that—always worrying, watching your back every second, day after day.

"We knew the risks when we signed on. But Kurtis wasn't a bargaining chip. When I started getting kidnapping threats, I knew it was time to come home so my son could live a normal life."

What could she say? Anything she had suffered during his absence was nothing compared to what he had gone through on a daily basis. And to have his son's life threatened—she knew what it was like to lose a child. But it still didn't justify his actions now. Their relationship was in the past.

"Katie, I want you to know how much you meant to me, how much you still mean to me."

His hands reached for her, she didn't resist. Couldn't.

"I hope you can forgive me for walking away and leaving you behind."

He pulled her into his arms, and once again all the old feelings washed over her. He lifted her, then gently knelt and laid her on the floor next to the fire. His lips covered hers—and she was lost in a dream where they had never parted. His touch, his scent, his tenderness filled her aching soul. Her toes curled when his hand slid under her sweater and cupped her breasts, again. Her heart stopped, and she held her breath. She clung to him, her arms around him, her head curled into his neck, her lips melting into his warm skin. The stubbles of his hair hypnotic as she unconsciously rubbed her fingers through the short strands. It took her a dazed minute to recognize that his fingers were fumbling with the snaps on her jeans. Wanting more from Mark, to continue to soak up the memories of his love-making, to regain the sexual fulfillment from so long ago, she reached down with her left hand to help him. Her diamond engagement ring caught on his shirt, pulling at it, and brought her to her senses.

What the hell was she doing? Gads! How could she still be under Mark's spell so easily? Twice in one night? Good Lord, she was engaged to someone else? About to go to Norway to be with Sven? She was pathetic thinking what…she had no idea. Guilt washed over her, she'd never be able to look at Mark again. How could she face Sven knowing Mark could induce such deep sexual feelings for him again so easily?

"I can't do this, Mark. You have to go."

"I'm sorry, Katie." He kissed her forehead and rolled off her. "I don't know what came over me. I swear I wasn't looking for this to happen. I only wanted to talk—explain."

She remained on the floor, shimmied backwards against the sofa, hung her head in bended knees, and couldn't muster the nerve to face him.

"Just go, please."

He stood. She heard him slowly walk toward the door, then pause.

"Katie…"

She couldn't have answered if she wanted to. Her insides were in turmoil, and she wanted to curl in a ball and cry her eyes out. The door opened and clicked shut.

Only then did she find the energy to get off the floor and make her way to her bedroom, and flop on the bed. What was she thinking? She had almost made love to Mark Logan.

How in hell was she going to play elf to his Santa on Friday?

How the hell was she going to face Sven when she landed in Bergen on Saturday?

****

Mark pounded his fists on the steering wheel. Dammit! He'd crossed the line. Pushed her too far. Having her in his arms again after all these years was paradise. Feeling her soft skin, her heavenly, silky firm breasts in his hands, and her lips against his neck. Good Lord, if she hadn't stopped him, pulled away when she had, they would have made love. His insides clenched at the thought of being inside Katie. Loving her. She'd been with him right up until whatever-the-hell had stopped her.

Of course! She was engaged, and more than likely only been caught up in the moment. Like he'd been. It was high school all over again, when he hadn't been able to keep his hands off her, hadn't been able to get enough of her. He'd only made things between them more awkward. What an ass! He needed to back off.

Mark leaned back against the headrest. The inside of the car was frigid, his fingers stiff as he turned the key in the ignition and cranked the heat on high. Of course she'd caved—she felt sorry for him. Losing his wife, dealing with being a single parent.

He stepped on the gas and pulled into the street. Dammit, he'd laid it on too thick—he hadn't meant to. He only wanted to explain why he hadn't contacted her all these years. And, yes, dammit, ease his guilt. Seeing her again had his heart racing—hoping he had a chance to mend the gulf between them. He hadn't counted on how beautiful she'd become. How independent and caring. And engaged! Why he thought she'd still be available when he had left her behind, made him nothing short of a moron. She deserved better. He hoped her fiancé appreciated Katie's love, devotion, and faithfulness.

He'd been too young back in high school, too full of himself, thinking he could make a difference in the world. What he'd done was make a mess of his life.

****

Katelyn's guilt filled every inch of her shaking, sobbing being. How could she let Mark get to her like that? She was engaged to Sven and had been about to make love to Mark. She went back to the living room, unplugged the tree lights, put the fire out in the grate, and made sure everything was shut off and locked for the night. A coldness enveloped her as she made her way to the bedroom—this time slower. Going to Norway was more important now than ever. She had to prove to herself that her love for Sven was strong enough—that it was a lasting love to withstand the draw Mark's return to Lobster Cove had on her heart. She couldn't wait until Friday to hop a plane, meet Sven in Bergen, and renew their commitment to each other.

She changed into her pajamas, crawled under the covers, flicked the lamp off, and sighed as her head hit the pillow. She shut her eyes, but sleep evaded her. How in the hell was she going to play a happy elf to Mark's Santa for the kids at the Christmas party on

Friday? She couldn't let Linda down. She couldn't let the children down, either. The only consolation making any sense, right now, was that she'd be flying to Bergen Friday night and wouldn't have to face Mark at daycare again—thankfully her class project ended on Friday immediately following the party.

When the phone rang at five the next morning, Katelyn was blurry-eyed, her head pounding, and her mouth dry. She fumbled for the phone, shutting off the alarm clock at the same time, and swung her legs over the side of the bed.

"Hello."

"Katelyn? Are you okay?"

"Sven! You woke me. I'm fine. How are things in Bergen? How are your grandparents?"

"Not doing so well. We need to talk, Katelyn."

"What is it, Sven? What's wrong? Oh, my God. Is it your grandfather? Has he taken a turn for the worse?"

"No, no, he's doing much better. That's not it. I don't know how to tell you this…but…well, I'm not going to make it home for Christmas."

"Oh, no. Sven. Christmas isn't going to be the same without you. I was so looking forward to sharing it with you as an engaged couple this year."

"I'm sorry, Katelyn. Things have sort of gotten out of control here. I need to reassess things. I can't walk away."

"I'm so sorry. I understand. I want to be there to help you through this difficult time."

"No. No. No need to worry. I'll let you know when I have things sorted out at this end. I'm really sorry, Katelyn."

She heard the concern in his voice, and was

troubled by the distance between them, glad she planned to join him. Should she tell him? She'd wanted it to be a surprise, but…

"What if I…"

"I've got to run. Dad wants me to check out my grandfather's company before he takes the helm. They have an appointment to meet with the office staff in about fifteen minutes. I really am sorry, Katelyn. I'll be in touch."

Had she just been given the brush off? Of course, he had a lot to deal with right now—a lot on his mind. But it wasn't like him to be so short with her. Maybe the situation was worse than she imagined and he wasn't able to talk about it over the phone. She knew that if her family was going through such problems, she'd certainly want to be there for them.

It was important now more than ever that she go to Norway and help in any way she could. It was the right thing to do. The more she thought about it, the more excited she became. Wouldn't Sven be surprised when she showed up on his doorstep? They could spend Christmas together after all.

****

Katelyn made it a point to be busy when Mark dropped Kurtis off Thursday morning. She kept watch from the library nook until he left—him and Connie, talking, smiling. She'd been right to pull back from him last night. She'd been caught up in the moment, trying to revive the past. She'd done them both a favor by stopping disaster taking control.

Linda was in the kitchen arranging the cookies and icing pots for the kids to decorate when Katelyn found her.

"Wow. Your mother did a fantastic job with the cookies. The kids are going to have a blast decorating these this morning."

"Actually, one of her chefs baked them. She assured me they were delicious. I haven't tried one yet." After talking to Sven this morning, she'd almost forgotten about them. They were on the kitchen counter where she'd left them the night before, but she had left the toppings in the car, overnight—thankfully they weren't frozen solid.

The next hour was spent trying to keep kids from eating cookies and licking icing from fingers, smearing each other with red and green food coloring, and making sure everyone had the same number of cookies to decorate. After the children were washed up, Katelyn settled them in the reading corner and read them stories while Linda cleaned the rest of the mess in the kitchen, and prepared lunch.

She loved reading to the kids. She was tickled when Kurtis made it a point to sit beside her. Like the others, he was very attentive and soaked up the tales and the antics she went through to bring the characters to life. In this digital age, it was encouraging to see kids enthusiastic about reading books. But it wouldn't do to single Kurtis out—the other kids would notice, and the repercussions could be harmful. It was important to keep their relationship low key until he was able to find his place with the other kids—showing favorites would not help.

Activities in the afternoon were just as frantic as the morning. Cutting out elf caps with red and green construction paper for tomorrow's party took patience with the smaller children using blunt scissors and colored markers to make designs and add their names to their caps. Later, they put the finishing touches on their parent's gift. Katelyn had spent time snapping pictures of each of the children, and printing them on the color printer so they could paste them on a background of poster board cutouts in the shape of a round ornament. The trickier part was for them to tie a red or green ribbon through the top loop so their gift could be hung on their family Christmas tree. Thankfully she had duplicates of the photographs, as some of the kids went a bit wild with the paste and smeared their pictures.

The afternoon disappeared, and before Katelyn was aware of the time, parents were arriving to collect their sons and daughters.

"What time should I plan Santa's visit?" Mark whispered in her ear as she helped Kurtis on with his coat.

Heat infused her face, her breath caught. Unable to look him directly in the eyes, she kept her head averted.

"Linda plans to start things at 11:30. While the children are having lunch, you can slip away and change."

"Katie…about last night…I…"

She had to stop him, it wasn't the time or place to have this conversation. "Please, Mark, let's not drag this out."

"Dad, I decorated Christmas cookies today. One broke so I ate it."

"Sounds like fun, bud. Come on, let's get your hat and gloves on. It's snowing."

Katelyn was relieved for the interruption, waved to Kurtis as he left, and finished helping the others with their snow outfits. How she was going to survive playing elf to Mark's Santa tomorrow was beginning to play on her mind. Could she do it? Or would she chicken out?

Later that evening, she packed her bags and placed them next to the front door so they'd be ready for the flight after the party. Katelyn prepared the house for her absence, trying to take her mind off Mark, the flight to Norway, and wondering what was going on with Sven in Bergen. She made sure the tree was watered, lights unplugged, and everything secured for the night. A sense of loneliness set in as she undressed and prepared for bed. Once under the covers, lights out, she lay staring into the darkness. A lone tear escaped. She shut her eyes, sent up a silent prayer heavenward that she was doing the right thing, and fell into a fitful sleep.

Chapter Nine

It snowed the night before the daycare's Christmas party, but the morning sky was clear and bright. Katelyn hoped the weather held for her evening flight. She decided to dress as a more casual looking elf, seeing as she wouldn't have much time to change before leaving for the airport afterward. She dressed in a pair of Kelly green slacks, with a black vest over a red turtleneck. She skipped the heavy clownish makeup, keeping it light and understated.

When she arrived at the center, all the daycare providers on hand also wore green caps, while some had dressed more festive with red or green blouses or sweaters. Parents started arriving at 11:30, but the children were already hyped up on excitement in anticipation of the party.

Mark arrived along with the other parents, nodded in her direction, and then joined the two fathers who had already arrived. Gerald Wolfe and Peter Gray were there with their daughters Megan and Emily, and although the three men congregated on and off, Katelyn wasn't surprised to see Mark and Connie pair off, smiles on their faces. Katelyn had mixed emotions as she observed their interaction with each other, and their sons. She loved how attentive Mark was to all the children—he was a wonderful father, and made a great Santa. She should be happy he found someone who made him happy—that Kurtis would have someone close in age that would make a great playmate. She liked both Connie and her son.

A sigh escaped her lips as Mark slipped into the rest room to change into his Santa outfit. It didn't take him long, and when he came back out, he spotted her, walked over and whispered in her ear as if there had been nothing between them the other night.

"You ready to do this?"

"Yes. Linda has a sack of gifts hiding in the closet. There are name tags on all the gifts to make it easier to hand out. If you'll wait a second, I'll get it for you. You can go out the side door and come back in the entrance. Linda will be there to unlock the door."

Katelyn dragged the brown burlap sack from the closet. When she turned, Mark was by her side.

"I can take it from here, thanks. I'll meet you by the front door."

She should be relieved he wasn't making a big deal out of the other night, but the ache within wouldn't let go. She had to remind herself that within hours she'd be flying off to surprise Sven in Norway. Help him with his family dilemma, and spend Christmas with him— something she'd been looking forward to all week. Funny—she didn't feel the excitement now that the day to depart had arrived.

Katelyn took her position just inside the door, waiting for Santa to enter. Linda joined her. The kids jumped up and down with excitement the minute he arrived. They rushed him, not giving him a chance to make it to his chair next to the tree the kids decorated with paper ornaments they had made during the week.

"Ho, ho, ho. Merry Christmas."

"Merry Christmas, Santa," the group shouted in unison.

Thankfully, Linda took over and herded the children to the floor mat in front of the tree, and had them sit horseshoe fashion so everyone had a birds-eye view of Santa. Katelyn stood next to the tree and the sack full of presents, waiting for Mark to take his seat.

"Let's get the party started," Santa told the group of sparkly-eyed kids, smiles beaming from ear to ear. "Miss Elf, may I have the first present, please?"

Katelyn reached in the bag, read the name on the gift and handed it to Mark. Megan was the first to sit on Santa's lap, followed by the rest of the children, while Linda snapped a picture of each of them on Mark's lap. Curious to see how Kurtis would react to his father playing Santa, she wasn't to worry, Kurtis was so taken by the red suit, and the gift Santa handed him, he didn't even notice it was his father. When he opened his present, he waved the hard-covered book on dogs in the air.

"Katie, look. Dogs."

"Your favorite animal." She smiled as he took his seat and started thumbing through the pages. It was the perfect gift.

When the last present was handed out, Santa stood, jingled his golden bells and said his goodbyes. The kids waved from their seats on the mats, and went back to playing with their gifts. Mark made a fast exit, rounded the corner and changed his clothes before coming back into the community room. A few of the mothers were busy arranging the luncheon, while Katelyn cleared all the wrapping paper and bows scattered on the floor, relieved for that portion of the program to be out of the way. Now if she could just get through the rest of the afternoon, the singing, the small skit the kids had been working on, and an attempt at remaining indifferent to Mark's attraction, and her embarrassment from their near lovemaking the other night.

The last hour stretched on. Linda handed out the coats they'd received from St. Joseph's Ladies of the Rosary Society, the last of the cookies were bundled into packets for each child to take home, and finally the parents gathered their children and they all went home. Mark, Connie, Kurtis, and Jason left together. Not surprised, Katelyn let a big sigh escaped her lips.

"You don't have to stay to help clean up this mess." Linda came up behind her. "Everyone was great at helping before they left, so there isn't much to do. You go on and get out of here—you don't want to miss your flight. Go, enjoy yourself. Get some rest on the flight so you'll be ready to surprise Sven. And be sure to let me know how things go. Oh, Katelyn, how romantic—straight out of one of those romance novels our local author writes."

"Not that steamy, I can assure you. But, yeah, it is sort of romantic, I guess." So why wasn't she feeling romantic, and instead was doubting whether or not she was doing the right thing?

"So, go. Get. Go surprise your man."

"Thanks, Linda. Are you sure you don't mind? I want to take a minute to stop and see my parents before I head to the airport."

Linda wrapped her arms around Katelyn and gave her a big bear hug. "Aw, Katelyn, I wish you all the best—now, go. Get out of here."

After a quick stop to say goodbye to her parents, Katelyn ran home, jumped in the shower, dressed and headed to the Hancock County Bar Harbor Airport in Trenton. The short flight would take her to Boston, where she'd catch the overnight flight to Norway. By the time she finally boarded, stowed her carry-on, and settled in her aisle seat for the transatlantic flight, her excitement turned to relief.

However, she was too keyed up over the last few days' events to sleep when the lights were dimmed. She had no interest in watching one of the many movies she could choose from on the screen in front of her. Instead, she kept watch of the GPS location of the jet as it soared across the earth's surface, and the Atlantic Ocean. Excited to actually be flying half a world away by herself, for the first time, to surprise Sven, she let the doubts set in.

The night flight was long and drawn out, which allowed Katelyn plenty of time to rethink her life. Having Mark come back to Lobster Cove, seeing him, touching him, kissing him, almost making love again, brought those emotions she'd had for him in high school tugging at her heartstrings. Thinking he interested in her again, then seeing him with Connie, was a wakeup call. Those feelings were in the past; she was engaged to Sven. She was on her way to be with him. She had been looking forward to getting married, and having children of her own—with Sven. No, she *was* looking forward to being married to Sven.

But were her feelings for Sven strong enough to overcome her high school infatuation with Mark? She needed to see Sven, talk to him, and be held in his arms—to confirm she was doing the right thing. Perhaps she and Sven would move to Bergen to live with his family after they were married. Sven wasn't sure what he planned to do. They needed to talk. It was an omen from above that a seat happened to be available on this flight. She was meant to join Sven and strengthen their bonds. Her excitement propelled her to put all doubts behind her.

She dozed fitfully, ate little, and tried once again to get engrossed in one of the many movies offered on the miniature screen on the back of the seat in front of her. Even the music stations held no appeal and only frayed her taut nerves.

She'd talked to her mother before she left, and had promised to call as soon as she arrived in Norway. Both her mother and father were excited for her, even though she might not be home for Christmas.

"Are you sure this is what you want, dear?" Her mother had hugged her. "I know Mark is back—are you concerned you still have feelings for him?"

"I'll admit seeing him again has opened up old wounds," she'd confided.

"Have you talked to him, yet—told him about the miscarriage? How you feel?"

"I thought about it. But I don't think it's necessary at this point—there's nothing to be gained by dredging up the past."

"Then you need to go to Sven, if that is who your heart says you need to be with."

"It's what I need to do. We're engaged. Besides, Mark is seeing Connie Blye."

"Are you sure they aren't seeing each other because their sons have become friends?"

"It doesn't matter, Mom. I'm committed to Sven. I'll work this out."

"All right, then, give our best to Sven. And remember, honey, this is the opportunity of a lifetime. Enjoy the experience. Send us a postcard, and call the minute you get there."

****

The small airport in Bergen was decorated for the yuletide—a welcome sight after her restless flight. She hit the ladies' room while she waited for luggage to be unloaded, and then made her way back to the carousel where she grabbed her small suitcase that was about to go around one more time. Going through customs was a snap, and before she could blink, she was in the small main lobby, which was more of a holding area. Having had a light breakfast on the flight, she wasn't hungry, even though it was now lunchtime in Norway. She slipped her coat and scarf on, pulled her suitcase behind her, and exited the building. Finding a taxi waiting outside, she gave the cab driver the Olsons' address and settled in the back seat. Thankfully, he understood English, and after he tucked her bag in the trunk of the car, they were headed toward Bergen.

The taxi passed through the streets where many of the more upscale shops were located. Strings of white lights amidst green garlands and large star-shaped decorations she assumed would be illuminated at night, were draped overhead. Other streets sported strings of white lights intermingled with greens and a trio of large red hearts at equal intervals. Storefronts were also festooned with garlands of green, some even had small lighted trees over the entrances to their shops. Passing by the main square, Katelyn's Christmas spirits soared.

Who could miss that tall tree in the square blanketed in a gazillion white lights already lit, and several shoppers carrying packages, children lingering, and families filling the square socializing—her heart overflowed with wonder. And it reminded her of home and the tree in the town square. She would miss the caroling at the gazebo back home. She loved Lobster Cove at Christmastime and was going to miss all the fun and excitement. But being by Sven's side now was more important than missing one Christmas with her family in Lobster Cove.

The taxi rounded the harbor, the fish market, the line of sharply peaked store roofs decorated with more white lights. Pedestrians were bundled in their winter attire, rushing in and out of shops. A light dusting of snow blanketed the ground. It was a scene she could only describe as a Dickens' Christmas here in Norway. The harbor area was larger than Lobster Cove, but reminiscent of home, nevertheless—a sharp stab of nostalgia tripped her heartbeats into overdrive.

The taxi driver swung the vehicle around at the end of the highway, along the coastline. Frozen-looking whitecaps in the fjord made Katelyn shiver. They headed up the hillside behind the harbor where crowded homes spread out along the hilltop overlooking the town below. Another five minutes and the cabbie pulled to a stop in front of a large steep-roofed cottage with a wooden picket fence. The open gate in front of the sidewalk appeared welcoming. Perhaps a good omen, after all.

Katelyn smiled as she accepted her luggage, thanked and paid the cabbie, and then made her way to the front door. A simple green garland highlighted the doorframe—a spray of evergreens attached to the entrance held together with a red bow. A handmade stuffed cloth heart dangled from the center. Fresh pine scent permeated the front porch. Katelyn breathed in the aroma, knocked on the door, and waited several minutes, wondering if anyone was home.

Mrs. Olson opened the door—and gasped.

"Katelyn! What are you doing here?"

Mrs. Olson's raised brows, wide eyes, hands clinging to her ample chest, not to mention her dismayed tone of voice, was a sure sign she was more than startled to find her standing on the other side of the door. Katelyn hadn't thought about what impact her showing up out of the blue would have on the Olsons. She wondered, not for the first time, if she'd made a mistake in coming to Norway without letting someone know of her plans. She had only contemplated surprising Sven. She hadn't considered his parents. Or, oh, no! His grandparents!

Katelyn tried to make the best of a difficult situation.

"Hello, Mrs. Olson. Is Sven here? When he talked to me the other day he said he wasn't able to make it back to Lobster Cove, so I thought I'd surprise him and join him here in Bergen for Christmas."

"Oh, my dear, I'm so sorry. He's not home at the moment. He's visiting ah…a friend. Where are you staying? I'll let him know where he can contact you."

"Hmm…well…ah…I decided to come at the last minute so I didn't have time to make reservations. I assumed Sven could help me with arrangements once I arrived." Katelyn shoved her hands in her pockets, her fingers starting to tingle as a touch of frigid air blew in off the harbor, and doubt settled in.

"You might as well come in out of the cold until you can make arrangements. We're about to have dinner. You can join us."

Mrs. Olson's strangled tone and worried expression was unusual, another sign she wasn't happy to find Katelyn on their doorstep. She was visibly displeased at her sudden appearance. If she had a place to go right now, she'd wish them well and leave. As it was, the taxi was long gone, and she was starting to feel a cold penetrate her body that had nothing to do with the weather.

"Thanks, but I see this is a huge surprise. I'm so sorry to be an inconvenience. If you'll recommend a hotel, I'll settle in there and wait to hear from Sven."

"Don't be silly. You're very welcome to join us. I'm sure Sven has filled you in on the situation here. It's just been overwhelming. Of course you're more than welcome. Where are my manners? Come. Mr. Olson and his mother are in the other room. Come in out of the cold and sit by the fire."

Puzzled at Mrs. Olson's formal manner, she pulled her lonely piece of luggage behind her, embarrassed to have imposed, especially at lunch time. She placed the black case behind the door and followed her future mother-in-law into the sitting room. And caught her breath. It was like stepping into Christmas past. The Olsons' sitting room's old-fashioned fireplace spanned a large portion of the room, a glowing open fire adding a brightness to the organized clutter, evergreens, various candles, pictures and knickknacks lined the mantel and vines hung along the side of the hearth. A floor-to-ceiling tree decorated from top to bottom with small white lights stood in the corner. Decorated to the hilt with bright glass bulbs, beads, and a myriad of homemade items glittered, the flames from the grate making it shimmer.

Pulling herself together, she looked around the rest of the room and found Mr. Olson, and an older, white-haired woman dressed as if she were going out for tea, sitting on a love seat opposite a large round oak coffee table. Several small comfortable chairs were arranged in a semi-circle in front of the fireplace. Children's antique toys littered every nook, crook and cranny. It was a cozy room.

"Well, hello, Katelyn. What a pleasant surprise." Mr. Olson stood. "Welcome to Norway."

"Thank you. I'm afraid I've come at an inconvenient time. I apologize."

"Nonsense. Come in. Come in. Have a seat. Mother, this is Katelyn Sullivan. Sven's friend from Lobster Cove."

Katelyn didn't miss the fact he hadn't referred to her as Sven's fiancée. She was starting to get real bad vibes.

"Miss Sullivan," Sven's grandmother said, rising from her chair. "How nice to meet you. And to come all this way to visit Sven and his new fiancée. Please have a seat."

Katelyn fell into the nearest chair. Had she heard correctly? Surely not. The poor woman must have gotten her thoughts confused, what with her husband in the hospital. She looked at Sven's parents waiting for one of them to correct the woman. Instead, neither could meet her eyes. They focused on anything in the room but her. What the hell was going on? Where was

Sven? Legs and hands shaking, she stood, glad she hadn't taken her coat off yet. She had to get out of here before she said or did something stupid. *Crap!*

"Please, excuse me. I think I made a mistake." A huge mistake if Sven's grandmother knew what she had just intimated.

"My dear, I'm so sorry," Sven's mother said. "I was under the impression Sven had already spoken to you." Which explained Mrs. Olson's surprise when she'd answered the door to find her standing there. "Please sit down—catch your breath."

There was no way she was going to remain in the room only to be pitied.

"Oh, dear, Inge, what have I done?" Sven's grandmother said, her hands twitching in her lap, her back straight, and an apologetic expression on her lovely face.

"Nothing, Mother. It seems our Sven has some explaining to do—sooner than expected, I imagine." Mr. Olson patted his mother's hands. "This is not your fault."

"If you'll excuse me, I must make hotel arrangements," Katelyn called over her shoulder on the way to the front hall.

"Katelyn. I apologize for my son." Mr. Olson stood, looking as if he wasn't sure what to do. "Of course we'll help you find a place to stay—at our expense. It's the least we can do, considering."

"Thanks for your offer, but I'll manage." And she would. Somehow. And without Sven and the Olsons. She needed to escape before she ran into Sven. Because, honestly, she didn't know what she would say. She wasn't ready to listen to whatever drivel he had to offer in his defense. His cool phone calls were beginning to make sense. She had to get out of there before he came to lunch with his current fiancée, most likely the friend he was visiting. How embarrassing. On the other hand, she'd like to tell him exactly what she thought of him right about now. He could have saved them both a boatload of grief and heartache if he'd just called it quits over the phone. No wonder he'd been so short with her. Putting her off. The jerk.

She had no idea where she was going, but headed for the front door. Perhaps the taxi driver would have a hotel recommendation.

"My apologies for foolishly putting you all in this awkward position. Tell Sven there is no need to contact me."

She opened the door...and froze.

"Katelyn!"

Sven's shocked voice and expression as she stood immobile, trying to take it all in—him and his new fiancée standing on the other side of the door—was priceless. And well deserved. She was glad she hadn't missed seeing the shame spread all over his handsome, but red face. The color suddenly drained clear down below his loose neck scarf. The woman on his arm stared at Katelyn as if she was a gnat that needed flicking off her shoulder. Damn. The woman was beautiful. And here she was looking like a bag lady without a home after the long sleepless night spent on the plane. She didn't need this.

"Hi, Sven." She took a deep breath, let it out between clenched teeth, and unloosened her tight fists. "Surprise, surprise."

"Katelyn!" he repeated needlessly. "What are you

doing here?"

Her insides shook, she gritted her teeth, and held her temper in check. But she couldn't contain it past the count of ten.

"Obviously not what I had in mind. So much for feeling sorry for you in your 'time of need'—you and your family's. You're such a chicken shit, Sven. Now, get the hell out of my way." She went to walk past him, but he blocked her path.

"We need to talk." He turned to the woman at his side. "Excuse us, Marta. Go join the family in the sitting room. I'll join you shortly."

The doting Marta thankfully remained silent, but gave Katelyn a sly look before going to the other room.

"Please. Let me explain," Sven implored.

He reached for her. Katelyn side-stepped his flailing hands. She didn't figure she'd be able to remain calm if he so much as touched her right now. On the one hand she couldn't wait to hear his trumped up explanations—on the other, she almost didn't want to hear a word he had to say. How long had he been deceiving her? OMG! Was this why he'd been dragging his feet about setting a date for their wedding this past year? She'd come all this way—for nothing. She might as well listen to what he had to say, tell him goodbye, and get on with her life.

Resolved, Katelyn let Sven lead her down a short hallway to what was apparently his grandfather's study. A large wooden desk, equally large bookshelf behind it, against the wall, and a matching filing cabinet in the corner dominated the room. Once the door shut, her eyes focused on Sven and the rest of the room's contents ceased to exist. He reached for her again—she recoiled from his touch. Unable to look at him any longer, she walked to the window and concentrated on the view of Bergen's Harbor far below in an effort to calm her trembling insides. A massive ship reminiscent of a marauding pirate vessel, sails unfurled and extending to the pristine sky, was tied up at one of the docks. A ferry/cargo/cruise ship was just pulling into the harbor, and people lined the dock waiting to meet the passengers. She wished she was on it. Anywhere but standing in Sven's grandfather's study covered in embarrassment.

"I'm so sorry you came all this way, Katelyn."

Sven's pleading voice snapped her out of her contemplations. She turned sharply from the window.

"So am I."

The shame on Sven's face, in his eyes, didn't pacify her. Was he only sorry she had come to Norway? Or that he had cheated on her?

"What a fool I was, thinking I was coming to your rescue. Is your grandfather really sick? Or was that something you fabricated to make me oblivious to what has evidently been going on behind my back?"

"He's still in the hospital."

He ran his hand through his already wind-tossed hair. His hand shook. Good. This wasn't easy for him. It definitely wasn't easy for her.

"When were you going to tell me—break our engagement? Were you even planning on coming home for Christmas?"

He didn't answer immediately. Guilt flashed in his eyes—he lowered his head.

"Your silence is answer enough." She would never be able to enjoy Christmas ever again.

"I didn't want to break it off over the phone," he finally spoke.

She almost didn't hear him. His voice low, as if he was talking to himself.

"So thoughtful of you. It would have been preferable, rather than finding out like this."

"I didn't mean for you to find out this way."

"Obviously!"

"How was I to know you would jump a plane and come to Bergen?"

"Again, obviously!"

"That's not what I meant. I was planning on flying back next week."

"Not necessary now. What a Christmas present! Thanks for nothing. Thanks for ruining Christmas for me—for ruining my life." She walked to the door, her head high, only to realize she still didn't have anywhere to stay, and needed to make flight arrangements to go back home. She had nowhere to spend the night. If she couldn't find something, she'd simply sleep in the airport until she could catch a flight back home.

"Goodbye, Sven."

"Wait, Katelyn. Please, let me explain."

Did she want to hear all the sordid details?

"Call me a cab and make reservations at a hotel, first."

"Yes, of course." He strode to the desk and picked up the phone without a backward glance.

Tears formed, she turned, and wiped at them, not wanting Sven to see how hurt she was at his quick acceptance of her wanting to leave. His hopeless, forlorn expression when he turned from making the call did little to make her feel sorry for him. Nor did it make her feel any better, damn him. She was the one who had been wronged, cheated on. Guilt looked perfect on him.

Her worst Christmas ever!

"You know what, Sven? I don't want to know all the gory details after all. It's not going to change a thing. Let's just leave it as is." She was letting him off the hook, but honestly, there really was nothing to be gained by sitting and listening to words that weren't going to make things right in the end, anyway. "I'll need the name of the hotel for the taxi driver. If you would be so kind as to write it down for me." She wanted to rant and rave, tell him what an ass he was, that she never wanted to see him ever again. But that would only make him feel justified in not having told her in the first place. As much as she wanted to, she stood quietly until he wrote the address on a piece of paper and handed it to her. "Tell your parents goodbye for me. I'll wait outside until the taxi arrives."

"Katelyn." He shook his head and stepped toward her. She stepped back.

"Don't."

"I'm..."

"Don't say a word."

"Let me come with you. Help you settle in at the hotel."

She could only stare, mouth open, brows raised in surprise.

"Too little, much too late. Don't drag this out and make it any harder for me." She turned and walked out the office door, grabbed her suitcase waiting in the front hall like a forgotten child, and shut the door behind her. He hadn't even tried to stop her.

Definitely her worst Christmas ever!

Chapter Ten

Sven might just as well have ripped her heart out of her aching chest. So much for surprising him and thinking it was so romantic. Well, the surprise was all hers. Coming all the way to Norway to be dumped on a doorstep bordered on the surreal. Angry as hell was too mild an expression. She was livid. It hadn't escaped her noticed just how much she resembled his new fiancée, either. The woman was fair skinned, had the same long blonde hair, was reasonably tall, and had a thin frame. But unlike her, this woman's boobs were well endowed. No doubt about it, Sven had most certainly been drawn to her because she looked so much like Marta.

Katelyn was glad of the warmth of the taxi as she settled in the back seat for the ride down the hillside to the hotel where Sven had made reservations. The Royal Blue Hotel was located behind the colorful row of two-hundred-year-old wooden houses from the Hanseatic time—her cabbie informed her in perfect English as they drove along the pier. "So close to the fish market. You must visit," he told her. She wasn't interested in visiting a fish market, or any other historic site, right now. She just wanted to settle in her room, finalize flight arrangements to go home to Lobster Cove, and pretend this never happened. She'd think about sightseeing later. Maybe.

The taxi driver drew up to the hotel portico,

jumped from the car, and retrieved her bag from the trunk. She stepped out of the vehicle, dug in her purse for tip money, and exchanged the tip for her bag. Sven had prepaid the cab fare. She went inside in search of the reservation desk. The interior was very modern, spacious, and decorated for the holiday. Several easy chairs and sofas were arranged conversational style with tables close by in the main foyer. The décor spoke of elegance with an open carpeted mezzanine staircase in the center of the opulent room, crystal chandeliers, and vivid seasonal sprays of flowers scattered around the foyer. Guests were in various stages of coming and going. She checked in, retrieved her room key, was given the hotel talk about the restaurant, the bar, the elevators, and ten minutes later was on her way up to the sixth floor, and finally her room.

Once inside, Katelyn deposited her suitcase next to the door, and plopped on the bed. She didn't bother taking off her coat. She was exhausted. Alone in a foreign country, minus a fiancé, was not how she had envisioned her exciting romantic adventure to play out. She was holed up in a hotel room, alone, not knowing how she was going to get home, or when. She simply gave in, shut her eyes, and fell asleep.

Two hours later, Katelyn woke, took a shower, and put on clean clothes. She drew the curtain aside and was greeted with a vivid blue sky, the late afternoon sunshine, a rumble in her stomach, and a new determination. Enough was enough. Sven wasn't going to take the excitement of Christmas completely out of her soul. She would get something to eat—at the fish market—and then do some Christmas shopping for her parents.

Katelyn walked out of the hotel and headed along those historic homes and shops along the wharf the cabbie had mentioned. The air was brisk, but not frigid, the sidewalk packed with locals and visitors shopping in the various novelty stores along the *Bryggen* District. She turned right onto Torget Street and headed for the outdoor fish market. Scaled back for the winter, vendors were scarce, but the ones selling fresh seafood were busy cooking for those who were brave enough to meet the elements.

Katelyn found a tented vendor, with a huge kettle of fish soup, steam rising, and a savory aroma of curry making her stomach crave whatever concoction the woman was selling. She dug in her purse for a few *Krone* she'd exchanged at the airport, accepted her large portion of curried seafood over white rice, then found a seat at one of the picnic tables under the tent— a small heater warmed the small enclosed area. Several locals sat at the other tables, enjoying their meals. After eating, she wandered back to the *Bryggen* area to check out the shops. The taxi driver had also mentioned the *Fløibanen* Funicular that would take her to the top of the *Fløyen* Mountain for a spectacular view of Bergen. Why should she miss out on at least one Norwegian adventure while in Bergen just because Sven had shattered her heart and her trust in men.

It was a beautiful winter's day, the sun kissed her face and sparkled off the water. The view would be spectacular, the cabbie had promised. She paid the fare and hopped aboard the cog rail that ascended the steep mountainside. Once on top, she stood on the viewing platform along with half-a-dozen other visitors, and had a clear panoramic view of the city, the mountains, and the fjords. The cabbie had been right. It was amazing. She tugged her scarf tighter around her neck, the wind having picked up in the higher elevation.

On top of the world, she looked out over the horizon toward home, and sighed. Despite the awesome experience, her heart sank. There was nothing for her back home, and there was nothing for her here, either. Even Mark had found someone else to take his wife's place. He and Connie Blye were evidently an item.

So what did that say about her? What was wrong with her? Why did men choose other women rather than her? What signs had she missed with Sven? He had dragged his feet, not wanting to set a date—should she have considered he didn't want to marry her? But then, he'd never mentioned he had a girlfriend back in Norway—and he had given her a ring. And Mark? What had really nudged them apart? And why had he kissed her and almost made love to her the other day, stirring remembered emotions, only to turn to Connie?

Several people entered the small café at the crest of the hill—she joined them, following the scent of strong coffee. She could use a cup of something warm to help dispel the chill that had set in while standing out in the cold. Instead of sitting at a table, she ordered a coffee to go, and took the funicular back down the hill. She sat in the very back of the vehicle where she had an unobstructed view of the fjords down below as they descended.

She sipped her coffee and let her mind wander back to seeing Mark again. His kiss had ignited a spark deep inside that had no business still burning—his presence in Lobster Cove reignited those feelings she thought had been laid to rest years ago. Memories of their high school graduation night flooded her entire being. Their love and subsequent lovemaking had been perfect. Mark had made her heart soar, astonished at how such a tough high school jock on the playing field could be so gentle and caring while making love to her. He'd been her first, and after the initial discomfort, he had taken her to heights she never knew existed.

She knew without a doubt that they would be together forever. A sadness washed over her as she recalled the results of their lovemaking—at first the shock that she was pregnant, the pleasure that she was having Mark's child, and then the anguish when she'd miscarried. She had never told anyone other than her parents—Mark had been long gone by the time she'd discovered they were going to be parents, and after she miscarried, there was no sense telling him—or anyone.

Katelyn sighed. She loved children and would have loved to have had Mark's child. And what a kick in the pants—Mark had a child of his own. Kurtis should have been hers. Tears flooded her eyes. She wiped at them. Her heart turned over wanting a child of her own.

Katelyn joined the others exiting the funicular, dumped her coffee cup in the trash, and made her way back to the shops along the quay. An hour later, arms full of Christmas packages for her parents, Katelyn entered the hotel lobby. And spotted Sven sitting in one of the comfortable lounge chairs, his coat unzipped, his scarf loose around his neck, and his eyes focused on the entrance.

Dear, Lord. What is he doing here?

Sven jumped from his seat and closed the distance between them. She clutched her packages tighter. She didn't want to deal with this—him.

"Are you okay, Katelyn? I couldn't let you leave Norway without knowing that you're going to be all right."

"I'm fine. I've given it some thought." Actually, she'd been thinking about Mark and how seeing him again had her emotions going haywire. Sven might have unknowingly done them each a favor. Would marrying Sven have been settling for second best? Still, he hadn't handled the break up very well—could have been more considerate of her feelings and been a bit more forthright over the phone. Then again, he hadn't expected her to show up in Norway, not giving him time to tell her. It was just as much a shock to him as it had been to her. Maybe she should have given him the opportunity to explain.

"I suspect neither of us is truly in love with each other." She sighed. Saying the words made her realize the truth. Her heart felt lighter. Maybe coming to Bergen was meant to be for a different reason than she intended.

Sven nodded, his lips tight, his hands shoved in his coat pockets. He looked as sad as she felt—they had shared so much these last two years, but neither of them was able to control their heart's desires. She was still in love with Mark. But it was too late.

"Let me buy you a drink. I know you didn't want to hear it before, but I'd like to explain. I didn't mean for any of this to happen."

"You don't have to do this. I think I understand."

"We need closure."

Closure? It sounded so mature coming from Sven. Or maybe she hadn't paid much attention after he'd given her the ring. *The ring!* Had he bought a new ring for his Marta?

"Thanks, I could use a drink. And you're right. We need to clear the air. Give me a minute to take these packages to my room."

"Let me help you."

"No. I've got it." She didn't mean to sound so sharp, but then, she hadn't expected to see Sven again quite so soon. He clamped his lips tight. What did he expect? He'd just dumped her. To be fair, he needed to explain, and she wanted—needed—closure, too. "Give me a minute, I'll be right back."

"The hotel has a bar—we don't need to go out, even though the weather has been mild the last couple of days."

After dropping her packages on the bed, she removed her coat, ran a brush through her hair, and slinging her purse over her shoulder, she headed back to the lobby.

Sven was waiting, and escorted her toward a corner table in the well-appointed bar. Within seconds, a waiter was at their table to take their order. As much as Katelyn considered ordering a double of anything— hold the rocks—she decided on a simple screwdriver. Appropriate, as she had just been screwed over by the man she was supposed to marry. And she had to travel half way around the word to find out he'd cheated on her.

She didn't even listen to what Sven ordered. But then, she really didn't care. The sooner they got this over with, the better. He could swagger himself right on back to his new fiancée. In fact, she really wasn't sure why she was being so nice and giving him the opportunity to appease his own guilt. She was ready to go home and get on with her life.

Sven kept looking over her shoulder as if watching, waiting for someone. Hopefully, it wasn't Marta. He fidgeted in his seat, and cleared his throat. Katelyn placed her hand over his, which was mauling the napkin the waiter had placed in front of him along with his drink. He finally looked into her eyes—his wide, expecting. She wanted to comfort him, take the sadness away. Not!

"Sven!"

"I'm so sorry, Katelyn. I had every intention of coming back to Lobster Cove. And to you. But when I came to Bergen, my father's announcement sent me into a tail spin. I didn't know which way to turn. I literally bumped into Marta after being told I was out of a home, a job, and no prospects to my name. My parents were selling everything and returning to Norway to live."

And she hadn't been there for him to turn to. Had she been, would they still be a couple?

"We, Marta and I, had a thing years ago," he continued. "When she asked me to go for a drink, I didn't think anything of it. One thing led to another, and…well…I was shocked to discover we still had feelings for each other—strong feelings. I know my grandmother called Marta my fiancée, but it isn't official. I couldn't do that to you. Not without talking to you first. Honest."

Katelyn took a long sip of her drink; the ice clinked in the frosted glass. She carefully placed it on the table, and proceeded to slip her engagement ring off her finger. She slid it across the table, all the while never taking her eyes off Sven. He stared as if mesmerized.

"Here. This no longer belongs to me. Maybe Marta would like it."

"You're unbelievable, Katelyn. You've got to be the most understanding, kind, and loveable person I've ever met. I've broken your heart and here you are thinking of me and Marta."

Yeah, she was a real saint.

"You make me sound like a Girl Scout who just earned her gold star."

"You deserve one."

If she was so loveable, why had he fallen in love with someone else? Why had neither he nor Mark loved her enough to stand by her instead of someone else?

She raised her glass to trembling lips—she should have ordered a double something to drink. She needed it.

Sven looked at his watch. She took another sip, drained the liquid, and then set her glass on the table. This was it. He'd had his say and was about to leave. Was Marta waiting in the wings for him? More than likely.

Sven rose to leave, hesitantly extended his hand toward her, as if he was afraid to touch her, afraid his own feelings for her would resurface. She was tired of pulling back. Tired of hiding her true feelings. But Sven wasn't the one she needed to confide in—to open up to, and confess to. She needed to talk to Mark. She stood, as well, his hand felt cold and unattached in hers.

"Sven. I'm not happy things turned out this way, but, like I said earlier, you did us both a big favor. Neither one of us wants to be married to someone we don't love. Let's leave it at that. You need to go, and I have travel arrangements to finalize—I don't want to miss my flight home."

"Katelyn…"

She wasn't prepared for the kiss. Thinking he was going to give her a simple peck on the cheek, she was startled when he pulled her in for a deep kiss, his lips fully covered her mouth. For a split second the familiarity of his lips on hers, his touch, lit a spark deep inside. The longer the kiss continued, however, the more the spark fizzled and died. She knew it was truly over between them. He released her, stepped back, and sighed. His eyes revealed the truth of it, as well.

It was over.

"Bye, Sven."

"Katelyn…"

"Don't. Just go. I hope your grandfather has a speedy recovery."

He walked out of the hotel. She sat, ordered another drink, and wondered why there were no tears. In fact, she felt nothing at all.

****

The early morning flight was full. Katelyn found her seat, stowed her packages in the overhead compartment, and slid in next to the window. It wasn't long before an elderly business man and his wife settled in next to her. After a brief smile, hello, and a nod, he had his laptop out and was down to business before the seatbelt light clicked on. His wife had her e-reader out and had settled back in her own world. Which left Katelyn with time on her hands to think about her pathetic life.

How was she going to tell her parents Sven had found someone else—dumped her like leftover meatloaf? Yes, her parents would be supportive. They

148

always had been. Especially when she had suffered the pain and anguish of her miscarriage. She couldn't have asked for more understanding, loving, and caring parents. But she wasn't looking for sympathy. She was older, now, and determined to deal with whatever life threw her way on her own. She hadn't anticipated this bombshell, however, and could certainly use a hug or two.

Her romantic holiday with Sven and his family had blown up in her face. Except for the smug expression on Sven's fiancée's perfectly made up, stunning face, the woman had the decency to keep her mouth shut and not make the breakup more agonizing than it had been.

With two men turning their backs on her, Katelyn dug deep inside her soul—where had she gone wrong? Despite what Sven said about deserving a gold star, she wasn't looking for a star no matter what the color. She wanted someone to love her in return—only her— someone to share her dreams, her life—a family. Was that too much to ask for in a man?

The flight was long. Again she tried to focus on one of the movies available on the screen on the back of the seat in front of her. She wasn't into horror or sci-fi, and the romance movies had her thinking of things she'd rather not think about at the moment—who needed a reminder of what she had just lost—was missing out on? Who needed to watch beautiful people making love when your own love life just went down the toilet? Even the music was too schmaltzy to listen to and only managed to put her in a deeper funk.

Tired from lack of sleep the past few nights, she couldn't get comfortable in her seat. She leaned against the narrow window frame and gazed for a time at the fluffy white clouds passing by. She thumbed through the Sky Mall Magazine from cover to cover, leafed through other magazines stowed in the seat pocket in front of her, picked at her meals, and excused herself to walk up and down the aisles to walk off her boredom, and her crappy mood. None of which helped.

Thankful when the jet finally landed back in Maine, she went through the motions of collecting her bag, dragging herself and her baggage through customs. It took her a few minutes to remember where she'd parked her car. Once everything was stowed, she didn't hesitate to point the car in the direction of Lobster Cove. And home.

Apparently the East Coast had had a snow storm while she'd been gone. The roads were plowed, the sidewalks shoveled, and the Christmas lights were on everywhere for the evening. There was little traffic, not unusual for a Monday night, so it didn't take her long to pull into her driveway, unload her luggage, unlock the front door, and walk into an empty house. She dropped the suitcase and packages on the floor. She didn't bother to turn her tree lights on. What was the use? She was the only one to see or enjoy them. Christmas was no longer her favorite time of year.

Chapter Eleven

Katelyn sat across from her mother at the kitchen table, Tuesday morning, tea cup in hand. The warm scent of ginger filled the spacious kitchen—a taste and smell of home and good times, and Christmas. A platter of her mother's delicious gingerbread cookies sat in the center of the table on a red Christmas platter. Her appetite might be whetted by the fragrance, but there was no way she would be able to swallow anything at the moment. Her mouth felt as if it was full of a dozen cotton balls sucking out all the moisture. How to tell her mother she and Sven were no longer engaged?

"So, dear, how was Norway?" her mother asked, placing a fresh pot of tea on the table. "I bet it was beautiful this time of year. Was it as cold there as it is here? I understand Disney used Bergen as a backdrop for their movie *Frozen*."

She hadn't seen the movie, so she didn't know for a fact, but after seeing Bergen, she could well believe it possible.

"Yes, Bergen was lovely. The fjords from the top of the hill overlooking Bergen were breathtaking." She waited for her mother to get the chit-chat pleasantries out of the way, knowing she really wanted to find out why she'd cut her trip short.

"Yet you cut your visit short. What happened? You don't look very happy."

That didn't take long. There was no way to sugar coat the situation.

"I know you've been hopeful that Sven and I would marry soon, and have a family of our own. I know you've been wishing that for me for a long time, but it isn't going to happen any time soon. Sven broke our engagement, and I gave him back his ring. In fact, he reconnected with a woman from his past, and according to his grandmother, they are now engaged."

"Oh, my dear. I'm so, so sorry." Her mother jumped up and scurried around the table, and pulled her into a big bear hug. The comforting touch ignited the waterworks she'd tried so hard to keep at bay.

"Oh, Mom. I feel like such a loser. First Mark, now Sven. What is wrong with me?"

"Nothing, sweetie. Don't you even think like that. There is nothing wrong with you. Circumstances always have a way of interfering and causing things to happen that aren't meant to be. What you need to do is follow your own heart and let it lead you—not let circumstances affect you."

Her mother handed her a tissue. She mopped her face, blew her nose, and hugged her mother, again.

"You're right, of course. I even told myself on the flight home I should talk to Mark, tell him about the miscarriage. I was a chicken when I had the opportunity the other day. I know it won't change anything, but at least I'll get it out in the open. Stop hiding it."

"You've been holding it in for a long time. You need to release all the old hurt—let the past go. The sooner, the better, no matter the consequences."

"You're right. You've always been there for me. What would I ever do without you and Dad? I love you both so much." Katelyn squeezed her mother's hands. Her mother kissed her cheek.

"We love you too, dear. You'll get through this. You'll see. We're here for you. We'll help."

It was time for her to talk to Mark—reveal her secret. If she could stand up and face Sven and his deception, and survive, she could face Mark. What did she have to lose, that she hadn't already lost?

****

Mark hefted Kurtis onto his shoulder and carried him from the Captain's Library to his car. His cell phone rang—he ignored it, and continued to buckle Kurtis in his car seat. He made sure his son was settled before he slid behind the steering wheel. Only then did he check his cell phone to see who had called. Damn. It was Katie. Where was she calling from? Linda had mentioned Katie had flown to Norway to be with her fiancé. Was she still there? Was she back home already? What did she want? He listened to the message, his eyes shut as her voice drifted into his ear, his insides—his gut tightened.

"Mark, I need to talk to you. Can you come over tonight after dinner?" There was a slight pause, and then, "Without Kurtis."

What did she want to talk about? Without Kurtis? His body warmed, and he hadn't even turned the heater on yet. She'd only been gone a couple of days, but he'd missed her. Was her coming back so soon a sign things had not gone smoothly in Norway? He could only hope. Her invitation had his libido soaring, wanting her, hoping it wasn't too late. Or was it only wishful thinking?

He checked his watch. It was only four. Plenty of

time to spend quality time with Kurtis before dinner and make sure he was safe at home with his parents. The kid was so wired waiting for Santa to arrive, he was a bundle of energy. Waiting patiently was part of his make-up—Special Ops had taught him how crucial patience could be, but he kept looking at the time—his watch, his cell phone, the clock in the kitchen—none of which helped speed time.

At 6:30, after dinner, and making sure things were secure, and Kurtis and his folks were settled for the evening, he said the hell with it and jumped in his car. Dusk had settled over the bay, the air chilled, but at least it wasn't snowing. The roads were plowed. He made his way across town.

Mark knocked on Katie's door, smiling in anticipation of her welcome. As soon as she swung the door inward and he saw her baby blues, he had her in his arms, kissed her hello before she could say a word. But damn, she looked so sexy with those long legs wrapped in black slacks, off-set by a fuzzy red sweater that accentuated her breasts. And her wheat-blonde hair hanging loose around her face—he had wanted to run his hands through those silky strands again—and again. But it was those deep blue eyes, bright and sparkly, that undid him, and had him reaching for her. His gut tightened. The kiss knocked him back on his heels. Or was it Katie who had just shoved him aside?

Her bright eyes looked more nervous than aroused. Tears? What the hell! He'd done it again. Overstepped, thanks to his raging hormones, and wishful thinking.

"Thanks for coming. Let me take your coat."

Yep! Her formal greeting didn't bode well. He handed her his coat, wiped his feet on the floor mat, followed her into the living room, and tried to think of something to say to break the ice and the uncomfortable silence. He ran his fingers through his hair and took a deep breath.

"It's beginning to look a lot like Christmas out there. Why aren't your tree lights on?"

At least she had a fire in the fireplace. The glow warmed the room.

"I haven't had time yet."

The sparkle in her beautiful eyes had disappeared. She looked tired, sad. Her face was pale and drawn.

"Let me take care of that situation for you." He bent down, plugged in the lights. The room transformed into a cozy holiday scene. There hadn't been much holiday cheer in his life since he'd left home for the military. Katie had unknowingly ignited that spark within.

"Mark, sit down. I have something to tell you."

"I'm so glad you invited me over, Katie. I need to apologize for the other night. For tonight. I just assumed…well, I thought…I…"

"Mark, please. You explained about you and Kurtis' mother. It's your turn to listen to me." She paused, took a deep breath, and then continued. "Remember graduation night when we drove to Cadillac Mountain and made love?"

"How could I forget? Memories of our night together kept me going for years. Holding you in my arms, making love with you. It was as if I'd died and gone to heaven that night."

"Me too. However…a month later, after you had already left for the military…" She choked back a sob. Telling him this was harder than she'd thought. He stood waiting while she wrung her hands. She shut her eyes, prayed for strength, then continued. "A month after we made love, I discovered I was pregnant."

"What!" He jumped up, swung around, shoved his hands in his slacks pockets, and then turned and faced her. "Are you sure? Why didn't you tell me? But where's the child? You didn't…"

"I miscarried. Mark, I was going to write and tell you, but by then there was no correspondence from you, no one knew where you were, and I didn't see the point. The only people who know are my parents."

"Damn it, Katie. I should have been told. You could have told my parents. They would have contacted me through the Red Cross. I can't believe you kept this from me."

She stood, faced him, her hands clasped at her waist, her shoulders back. Dammit. Her lips trembled, but her angry words flew at him.

"I didn't know what to do. I was eighteen, alone, and for all I knew—now know—you had moved on."

"Dammit, Katelyn…" He stopped mid-sentence. What could he say? He had disappeared, had a completely new identity, and had turned his back on his family for what he thought was an honorable cause. "For what it's worth, Katie, I never stopped loving you. I wish I'd known. I would have found a way to be with you. To be by your side."

He wanted to run his hands over her pale cheeks, brush aside the errant strands of hair that twined around her neck. But his gut wrenched at what he had unknowingly put her through. God, he was the worst ass. He turned, grabbed his coat from the back of the chair, and sprinted toward the front door. He had to leave before he took his anger out on her.

"Mark, wait…" She ran after him. He couldn't stand to see the disappointment in her eyes another second. He had to leave before he said something that would only make matters worse, and have her hating him more than she did already.

Mark drove out of Lobster Cove, the town lights fading in the rearview mirror. He didn't even notice when he drove off the island, and continued aimlessly, not heading in any particular direction. The sky was overcast, the night had turned as dark as his thoughts. Anger didn't even begin to describe how he was hurting. Talk about keeping secrets. How could she do this to him? How? Why hadn't she tried harder to find him, get word to him? Had she thought so little of him? That he wouldn't do the right thing?

It started to snow, light flakes that without warning turned into a swirling blizzard. He slowed, came to a town, a plow passing him in the opposite direction. He spotted the flashing lights of a fast-food diner and edged his car into a parking spot next to the building. He sat for a moment wondering what the hell town he'd pulled into. With the whiteout, the only way to find out was to get out of the car and go inside. At least get a strong cup of coffee and a caffeine fix to shake him out of his inner rant. And keep him awake long enough to find his way back home.

Mark ordered a burger, fries, and an extra tall cup of coffee, with one for the road. He found a seat facing the window where he could keep an eye on his car and the entrance. He scanned the typical fast-food restaurant's interior before he unwrapped his burger. He chewed without tasting the juicy sandwich, sipped his coffee, and then sat back. And thought about having just walked out on Katie. And then it hit him. What she must feel, knowing he'd married and had a son, while she'd lost a child. His child! She loved children. She loved Kurtis. God, it must be tearing her up inside, having to face the reality of it every day. No wonder she'd pulled away from him every time he'd kissed her. And then to walk out on her tonight—not staying long enough to comfort her, tell her he was sorry for what she went through—alone. And all he could think about was how hurt he was that she hadn't told him that she was pregnant with his child. *Way to go, asshole!*

He had to see her. Set things right. Was it too late? Would she talk to him, listen to him? There was only one way to find out.

The blizzard had turned into a small snow squall while he'd been inside and was nothing more than a light snowfall once again. He made his way to the car, put the coffee container in the cup holder between the seats, backed his vehicle out of the parking lot, and pointed it toward Lobster Cove. And Katie.

Hell, he had no idea if she was still engaged to that Norwegian.

With his mind focused on Katie, Mark managed to miss a turn, slide to a stop, missing a snow bank before he could get the car turned around and back on the road. The closer he got to Lobster Cove, the harder it snowed. An hour later he pulled up in front of her house. The house was dark, the tree lights he'd plugged in for her earlier had been extinguished. Mark glanced at the clock on the dash. Past midnight. He sat for a few more minutes, revved the car, and slowly eased onto the road.

Shit! He'd forgotten about Kurtis. One of the first

things he'd insisted on when he came home was a
security system at his parent's home. Only then could
he be sure his son stayed safe. Thank God, his father
and mother were vigilant—he'd filled them in on the
risks to his son, but it was his responsibility to make
sure Kurtis was safe. He'd let that slip, thanks to his
anger—not his usual MO.

His father was waiting for him in the sitting room,
watching the late news, when he made it home.

"Sorry I'm late, Dad. Everything okay?"

"Yes. Your mother checked on Kurtis before she
retired for the night. She spoils him."

"Like you don't." Mark smiled. His parents had
been over the moon to have him and Kurtis stay with
them until he could find a place of their own.

"How about you? Everything go okay tonight?"

"Not really. Think I've really messed up—again."

"You'll figure it out."

He'd been trying to figure it out since he returned
to Lobster Cove. And look where it had gotten him.
Lost in a snow storm—out in the cold.

Chapter Twelve

Wednesday night turned clear and star-studded. A perfect night for caroling at the town square. A slight breeze drifted off the cove, but it didn't stop the park from filling up to overflowing with carolers high on Christmas spirit. Katelyn found a parking spot next to the library, and sat in the car taking it all in. Colored lights strung around the entire parameter illuminated the festivities. The gazebo was decked out in garlands, red ribbons, and white lights, and everyone was bundled up for the weather.

She made her way to the gazebo along the crowded sidewalk. Kids romped in the snow, rolling snowballs to form snowmen for the snowman contest that would take place later in the evening. A small band inside the shelter of the gazebo pumped out Christmas music, while everyone joined the Community Chorus in song. "O Come All Ye Faithful" was just ending, followed by "O Tannenbaum." On cue, the Christmas tree in the center of the square was lit for the evening. The gaiety lifted Katelyn's mood—she couldn't help but smile, wave a hello, and even stop and talk with many of her friends and acquaintances. Linda was there with her husband.

"So, how was Norway?" Linda sipped her hot chocolate, warming her hands on the cup, her nose already red from the cold night air.

"A mistake. Or maybe a near miss. Depends on how you look at it." Katelyn scanned the crowd. "What a turnout."

"Uh oh. What aren't you saying?"

Should she tell Linda? She'd already talked to her parents. Why not? Everyone in Lobster Cove would find out soon enough.

"Seems Sven got himself engaged to someone else. Apparently a woman he's known and has been in love with on and off all this time."

"What? No way!"

"It was quite a shock."

An understatement for sure, she was still reeling over the surreal fiasco.

"I'm so sorry, Katelyn. Is there anything I can do?"

"Thanks, but I'll be okay. Great turn out tonight, huh?" She scanned the crowd. "One of the best in a long time. I think the weather has something to do with it, don't you?"

"Okay. I understand. No more talking about Sven. Yep. A great turnout tonight. A lot of the kids and their parents are here. And, they are wearing their new coats from the church. That was such a great idea. We'll have to remember that for next year, kids grow at such a fast pace at their age."

Katelyn wasn't sure what next year would bring—where she would be, what she would be doing. If she'd still be in Lobster Cove. She scanned the crowd again. There was Mark with Connie, and their two boys watching the older kids build snowmen. How could she face him today, after he'd slammed her own door in her face? He hadn't called, or tried to contact her. Her insides still burned from his anger. And there he was with Connie. They looked comfortable together. They looked like a family. She sniffed back tears. There was no way she could stay in Lobster Cove if Mark and Connie married.

About to turn away, Mark caught her eye. His smile was short lived, however, as Kurtis spotted her and ran to her side. Crap. This was going to be difficult. She couldn't ignore Kurtis just because his father hated her.

"Hi, Kurtis. Are you having fun tonight?"

"Katie. Snowman. Come see."

"I can see from here. They're big. You should have your father help you build one."

Kurtis looked at his father, who had ambled over, an expectant expression on his face. Mark smiled at his son. Her heart fluttered thinking what it would have been like had their child lived. If Kurtis was hers.

"If you'll excuse me, I'm headed over to Love Caters All for a hot chocolate." Katelyn used the excuse to escape the tense encounter.

"Hot cocoa. Want hot cocoa. Please, Katie."

Jason overheard, ran over, and added his plea to Kurtis'. She waited for Mark's approval. He nodded his head in agreement, just as Connie approached.

"Hi, Katelyn. These two bothering you?"

"Not in the least. I was just about to take them for a hot chocolate, unless you rather I didn't."

"No, that's fine with me. Mind if I join you?"

"Not at all." She liked Connie, and her son Jason was a sweetheart. How could she refuse either of them just because Mark had walked out on her?

Connie turned to Mark. "The Chief of Police is looking for you. He said he'd wait for you next to the

Lost Fisherman Statue."

The two young boys raced each other toward the pink catering truck, weaving in and out among the crowd. Katelyn dodged an elderly couple, then lost track of the boys—they'd been swallowed up in the excitement of the night.

"Do you see them?" she asked Connie.

Connie elbowed through the crowd, and then sprinted ahead. "Over here. They're by the trees. I'll meet you at the catering truck and get in line."

Katelyn was just about to collar Kurtis when a tall, burly man stepped in front of her. She bumped into him, keeping her eye on Kurtis.

"Sorry. I wasn't watching where I was going."

She heard his grunt, ignored it, and was about to catch up with Kurtis, when someone blocked her path, grabbed Kurtis' arm, and pulled him into the shadow of the trees. The man had on a black face mask, was stocky, tall, and held something in his right hand.

Katelyn lunged at the man's back with her left shoulder, and knocked him to the ground. Kurtis rolled to the side. She quickly lifted him into her arms, but before she took two steps, a second assailant's fist punched her cheek. She hit the ground, her hold on Kurtis loosened.

The man tried to pry Kurtis out of her arms, but despite the pain radiating through her head and down her neck, she clung to Kurtis and kicked out at the man's knees. He let go and fell to the ground with a groan. She stood, never letting go of Kurtis, his face buried in her chest, his grip tight, as she tried to run to safety. But the man was back on his feet and tackled her, pointing a gun at her temple. The cold hard pressure of it against her scalp scared her silly.

The man didn't hesitate and hauled her and Kurtis into his strong, muscular arms. In seconds they were shoved behind one of the buildings, out of sight from the crowd. A black van, with the motor running, was waiting close to the curb. The band playing and the carolers singing masked the sound. Before she could protest, regardless of the gun still aimed at her head, they were shoved in the back of the vehicle.

The door slammed shut before she could blink. A third man sat behind the wheel pumping the accelerator impatiently, waiting for the others to get in. Katelyn hung on to Kurtis and reached for the door handle only to have the doors automatically lock with a loud snap that sounded like a gun being fired. She could only hang on to Kurtis as the van sped down the street away from Mark.

Kurtis shivered in her arms. Her heart ached for what he must be going through. If she hadn't held on to him, he would have landed in this van full of kidnappers all alone. What the hell was Mark involved in that they were after an innocent child? It had to be something big if they followed him all the way to Lobster Cove, Maine. And, oh, Lord, she hoped Connie, who had been trying to catch up with Jason, had witnessed the attack. Had anyone seen them being thrown into the van? Whisked out of sight? She was going to have to figure something out—and soon. She couldn't let these thugs take Kurtis away from her. She didn't want to be responsible for losing both of Mark's sons.

****

"What's wrong? Where's Kurtis?" Mark's heart

lodged in his throat. He knew the answer. Daryl Johnson, Chief of Police had just finished filling him in on a security breach. Homeland Security had been trying to get in touch with him. *Shit! Shit! Shit! They had Kurtis! After all the precautions they had put in place, they still managed to find him and kidnap him.*

"They took them." Connie managed, trying to catch her quivering breath. "What's going on, Mark?"

"Them? You mean they took Katie, too?"

"Yes." She shook her head, pointing back at Love Caters All's pink van. "Two men with black masks grabbed them. It happened so fast, Mark, there was nothing we could do. Katelyn fought them, but it was no use. We tried to get back to you as soon as we could, but the crowd has grown thicker."

"Did they see you? They didn't follow you, did they?"

"No. I was chasing Jason. When I caught up with him, we were on the back side of the catering truck. They didn't see us. As soon as they left, we ran straight back to you. I'm so sorry, Mark."

"Go find Chief Johnson. Tell him what happened. Tell him I'm going after them. Then find someone you trust and hang out with them. Keep Jason with you."

He didn't give her time to respond. He had to find them before they put Katie and Kurtis on a vessel and disappeared. He punched in Homeland Security's number on his cell before he reached his car.

"They've got him. Katelyn Sullivan, too."

"We're on it. Go."

He had hoped it wouldn't come to this. Yet, deep inside his gut, he knew it was inevitable. Natasha's family was wealthy. Her child would pull in a hefty ransom, especially as payback for some of the more deadly ops she'd been involved in. A few of those ops made him a target as well. But none of them involved Katie, which meant they had no use for her. Dammit! He should never have come back to Lobster Cove and put her life in danger. He scanned the crowd as he sprinted to his car. He spotted his parents sitting on a bench next to the gazebo talking with the Sullivans. He headed in their direction. Shit! This was not going to be an easy conversation. He didn't have time for this, but it had to be taken care of now.

"Mom, Dad, Mr. and Mrs. Sullivan. There's no way to break this to you, but I'm glad you're all together. I only have a second."

"What is it, son?" His father stood, followed by the others.

"Oh, my God! Mark. Where's Kurtis? Did they take him?" His mother looked ready to faint. Her hand to her chest, she swayed into his father.

"Kurtis and Katie have been kidnapped."

"Katelyn? Kidnapped? My God! Roark!" Dawn Sullivan clutched her husband's arm.

"I have to go ASAP. I want all of you to stay together. I've instructed the security guards to escort the four of you to a safe place until this is over. Stay there until you hear from me."

He ignored their collective gasps as he fled the park, jumped into his vehicle, and headed for Bar Harbor. The bastards wouldn't have been so stupid as to dock at Lobster Cove with the Coast Guards being close by. What they weren't aware of was that Bar Harbor was on high alert, as was the entire Maine coastline and the Canadian border. Thanks to his new position with Homeland Security, they were all aware of such a possibility. Would they catch the kidnappers before it turned deadly?

Twenty minutes later, Mark pulled in next to the Bar Harbor docks, and jumped from his car. The Coast Guards, a handful of local police, FBI agents Jake MacKenzie and Ben Asher, and Homeland Security agent Gerald Wolfe, had detained and were in the process of handcuffing three men. He sprinted toward the commotion, breathing hard, looking for Kurtis and Katie. The Coast Guards were boarding an unassuming yacht, guns drawn. A helicopter hovered overhead. Blood pounded in his head. Was Kurtis already aboard?

From the corner of his eye he spotted a woman step away from the crowd. It dawned on him that it was Calla Hutchins, Petty Officer of the Lobster Cove Coast Guard. And then he saw him. Kurtis. She was holding Kurtis in her arms, and they were coming his way.

"Daddy! Daddy. I'm here, Daddy."

His son's arms reached for him. Mark didn't stop running until he had Kurtis in his arms. His son was safe. Thank God.

"You're okay, now, bud. I've got you." Mark drew him into his arms for a tight hug. He kissed Kurtis' temple, snuggled him under his neck. "You're safe, now. They didn't hurt you, did they?" His heart turned over as tears trickled down Kurtis' cheeks. He was safe. His son was safe. Thank God they caught the bastards before they'd smuggled him on board the yacht.

"Katie's gone. Daddy, the big man threw her out the door. She screamed. Loud."

More tears fell from his son's eyes. Tears formed in his own eyes. He clenched his jaws. How the hell had he let this happen? He wanted to kill the men who had done this to his boy. To Katie. Where the hell was she?

"Katie got hurt," Kurtis sobbed.

"We'll find her, bud. She'll be okay. Come on, let's go talk to the police." Mark hefted him in his arms, hugging him tight against his shoulders. He prayed Katie was still alive. Where the hell had they dumped her? And what condition was she in after they had pushed her out of their vehicle. Hopefully they hadn't shot her and discarded her body. The bastards! It was freezing out. She wouldn't last any length of time if she was still alive, lying somewhere along the shore. The nighttime temps had dropped rapidly since the wind chill coming off the Atlantic had picked up.

Gerald Wolfe approached before Mark could head their way.

"We need to put out a search STAT—a possible injury—have the hospital on alert," he called to Gerald. "Katelyn Sullivan was tossed from their van somewhere along the route—unless they went off-road to get rid of her. Not sure what happened, or what condition she's in. I'm taking my son and driving along the coastal route, see if I can find anything."

"We'll spread out from here—get another 'copter in the air. Keep the lines clear unless you find something. We'll want to get in touch with you."

"What about your son?" Calla asked. "Let me take him back to your parents."

"He's not leaving my side."

"Is that wise? He'll be safe with us, Mr. Logan."

"Not gonna happen. Thanks." He carried Kurtis to the car, buckled him in, and then drove to a fast-food joint with a drive-through and ordered a hot chocolate for Kurtis, and two large containers of hot coffee. He handed over the money, took a long swallow from one of the Styrofoam containers, and secured both cups in the holders between the front seats. He drove out of Bar Harbor, then pulled the car onto the coastal road at the foot of Acadia and hoped like hell he'd find Katie. He had to find her. He prayed she was still alive.

****

Katelyn lay dazed. What the hell just happened? And then she remembered and wanted to scream. Oh, my God! They had Kurtis. She'd failed to keep Kurtis safe from the kidnappers. If Mark didn't hate her before, he surely would hate her now. He would never forgive her. Dammit, she'd never forgive herself.

Where were they taking him? Why? What were they going to do with him? The poor boy. He was so scared, he'd clung to her, whimpering, as they pulled him out of her arms before they tossed her from their car. She could still hear his scream as the car drove off. Hopefully Connie had seen them being shoved in the van and got word to Mark in time to alert the authorities? Whatever Mark and his team did in such cases, she prayed they were expedient. They had to find and rescue Kurtis before something awful happened to him.

Small swirling flakes twirled down on her face. She wiped the snow from her eyes, only to have a pain shoot up her left wrist—she pulled back in shock. She moved her legs in turn—they were stiff but working. Surprising, after the way she'd hit the pavement before rolling into a frozen snow bank. She prayed her wrist wasn't broken. She propped herself into a sitting position using her right hand, caught her balance, and then stood. She dusted the snow off her jacket, and wished she had worn something warmer. She didn't know how long she'd been lying there, but the air blowing in off the ocean was frigid. She wrapped her scarf around her head, covering her ears, and then tugged it around her neck.

Stiff, sore, cold—it took a minute to determine her location, and figure out which direction she needed to head in order to get back to Bar Harbor and Lobster Cove. She had no idea what time it was, there was no traffic, and the once clear night had become overcast and hid the moon. It was difficult to see more than two feet in front of her. Once she decided on a direction, it was vital that moving forward was better than standing still, she took a deep breath and started walking.

Her cell phone was in her purse, which had been knocked from her shoulders when she had been grabbed. It was probably still lying in the hedge covered with snow. There was no means to contact anyone for help. She prayed a car would come her way before long so she could flag it down. With the way her luck was going, everyone was still enjoying the festivities back at the gazebo unaware of the kidnapping. When the community of Lobster Cove came together for an event, everyone showed up. They were no doubt still singing Christmas carols and having a wonderful time.

Did anyone know she and Kurtis had been kidnapped? Did anyone miss them?

The further Katelyn walked, the more depressed she became. Not only was she responsible for losing Mark's first child, she had lost his only surviving child.

Unless he survived the kidnapping. She sent up a prayer as she walked along the edge of the road, asking for guidance from above to save Kurtis from this horrid ordeal.

In the distance, lights flickered on the water—hopeless, despondent, and feeling a failure, Katelyn recalled her own ordeal of losing her child, and Mark's reaction to the news. And now Kurtis. She wanted to lie down, roll into a tight ball, and give in to the grief. But sobbing her guts out wasn't going to save either Kurtis or herself. Freezing to death wasn't going to solve anything, either. The few tears that did escape were like shards of ice on her cold cheeks. She tightened her scarf around her face as best she could, shoved her gloved hands in her pockets, and trudged on. Time stood still as she put one foot in front of the other. She had to keep moving. Progress was slow, labored. Her feet ached from the cold despite her warm fur-lined boots. Her teeth clattered, her whole body shivered. Katelyn tightened her clothing around her middle and blew hot air through her mouth into her icy hands. She wanted to sit down, rest for a moment.

Maybe just for a minute.

****

Had something—someone—moved up ahead?

Mark slowed, focusing on the spot where he thought he saw something dark shift alongside the road up ahead. He reduced his speed, drew closer, only to discover an area where the snowplow had pushed snow to the side, and was now covered in sand.

Nothing!

"Help me look, bud. Does this area look familiar? Did you drive along this road?"

"Don't know," Kurtis whimpered.

"That's okay. We'll find Katie, bud. Sit tight."

It was a long shot that Kurtis had seen anything, but it was worth a try. The poor kid had been traumatized. He probably should have let his son stay behind with the authorities, but he needed to have him close, make sure he was okay. And to give Kurtis the security he needed after what he'd gone through. He couldn't get the look of sheer relief on his son's eyes out of his mind, when Kurtis had spotted him.

He drove on, creeping along, searching in the dark for any sign of Katie. He drove around a bend in the road, scanning the area, looking out into the coastal waters. Was he going in the wrong direction? Had the kidnappers driven along this route? Maybe he should backtrack, go off-road. He rounded another bend in the road, and slammed on the breaks, and pulled over. A lone figure stood hunched over against the cold on the side of the road. He knew in an instant it was Katie! It had to be Katie!

He did a quick check of his surroundings to make sure they hadn't been followed, then double-checked Kurtis to make was he was secure in the back seat. He kicked up the heater on high before he exited the car on a dead run, locking the doors with the key fob. He was by her side in seconds.

"Katie. Oh my God. Are you okay? Are you hurt?" He didn't give her time to respond, he scooped her into his arms.

He kissed her forehead, her cold cheeks, and hugged her to him. He never wanted to let go. "I thought I lost you, too."

She came alive all at once, her eyes glazed, wide.

"Too? Oh, God. No! Kurtis? What happened? Where's Kurtis?"

Tears trickled down her cheeks. He wiped them away with the pad of his thumbs.

"Hush. He's okay. Kurtis is okay. He's in the car with me. Come on, let's get you inside where it's warm."

She leaned into him, he caught her. "Come on, love, let me help you to the car. You're shivering to beat the band. You must be freezing." He didn't want to think about how long she'd been out in this frigid weather. Had she been knocked out when they'd thrown her from the car? Lying on the side of the road in this god-awful weather?

"I'm f-f-f-f-ine. P-p-p-p-put me down, Mark. I c-c-c-can walk."

"I don't think so. You can hardly talk, let alone stand up straight."

"I can make it."

He set her down, slowly, until her feet reached the pavement.

"Katie! Katie!" Kurtis rushed from the car, and flung his tiny body against her quivering legs."

"Easy, bud. Katie's a bit shaky. We need to get her to the car, and get her warm."

"Katie, did those bad men hurt you?"

Katie disentangled her arms from around Mark, and dropped to her knees. She pulled Kurtis close. "I'm f-f-fine, honey. How about you? Did those awful men hurt you?"

"No. The police caught them and took them away. Then my daddy came. Then we came to find you."

"We're safe now. Let's go home."

Mark had all to do not to cry from relief at the sight of the two most important people in his life—safe. They were safe. His insides curled—he should never have come back to Lobster Cove and put their lives in danger. He kneeled next to them, wrapped his arms around them in a group hug.

"Back to the car, bud. I need to help Katie. Can you open the door for me?"

Mark did a quick check inside the car as Kurtis had left the door open when he got out. He wasn't about to chastise his son for this safety violation, but they would certainly have a talk later to discuss such issues. For now, he concentrated on making sure Katie was settled in the front seat. He checked to make sure Kurtis was secure, then wrapped the seatbelt around Katie, and locked the doors.

"Mark…"

"Hush. We'll talk later. I bought you a cup of hot coffee." He lifted the tab back from the sealed lip and handed it to her. "It's loaded with extra sugar. The hot liquid will warm your inner core and keep the outer cold from moving in and lowering your body temp. How are the feet? The hands?"

"The feet are cold, but okay. My wrist is a bit sore. I think I sprained it when I tried to break my fall when they threw me out of the van." She took a sip of the coffee he handed her and held the cup between her hands. He knew the insulated cup did nothing to help warm them.

He had done a quick check when he spotted her along the road—pleased her scarf covered her ears and face. The ears were always the first to be affected by the cold. Thankfully, it didn't look as if frostbite had set in. Mark knew the body would pull the blood back from the hands and feet to keep the core temperature elevated. The heater would take care of her feet, but she needed something for her hands. The hand warmers hunters used would be perfect, as would the lightweight, specially designed blanket he kept in the trunk for emergencies.

"We need to get you to the hospital, now, get you checked out for hypothermia. We'll have them check your wrist, as well."

"I'm fine. Really. Just a bit cold."

"Don't argue. I'll be right back." Mark made sure the doors were shut to keep the cold out before he rounded the car, opened the trunk, pulled out an emergency kit, grabbed what he was looking for, and then dashed back to Katie's side.

"Here, put these inside your gloves, they'll warm your hands faster than this heater." He snapped the packets, then handed her one for each hand. He unfolded the blanket and wrapped it around her.

"Daddy. Look. A 'copter."

Mark pulled out his cell phone on his way around the vehicle and stood outside the driver's side door while he punched in a number. It only took seconds for someone to pick up on the other end.

"I've got her, Gerald," he said. "We're on the way to the hospital. Call our parents and have them meet us there. But for God's sake make sure they know they're both okay. I don't want them to panic. Is everything under control at your end?"

"Roger that. Contact me the minute you get back to Lobster Cove. We'll wrap things up here, and touch base in private later."

"Thanks. Let the men in the helicopter know we're okay down here."

Mark looked up in the sky as the helicopter glided off toward Bar Harbor.

He got in the car, did a K-turn in the road, stepped on the gas, and sped toward Lobster Cove's hospital.

Chapter Thirteen

Mark pulled the car up to the emergency entrance. A wheelchair was waiting for her as she stepped out.

"I don't need a wheelchair. I can walk in on my own."

"That may be, but I'd prefer you let someone take care of you—get you inside out of the cold while I park the car."

As soon as she sat, she was whisked through the automatic glass sliding doors. She blinked, adjusting her eyes. The brightness of the stark white interior was blinding after coming in from the dark, overcast night. Mr. and Mrs. Logan swooped in, Mr. Logan lifting Kurtis into his arms. Mrs. Logan stood next to them, trembling, running her hands over her grandson's head in soft, gentle strokes as if he would break in two. She leaned in and kissed his cheek, then the three faded to the other side of the room.

Katelyn blinked back tears, only to shed more, as her mother and father rushed to her side, tears streaming down her mother's face, her father's eyes bright.

"Oh, Lord, Katelyn, we were so worried."

"I'm okay, Mom, Dad. Mark insisted I come, but I'm okay. Really."

Her mother leaned in and had her in a tight hug, her father's hand covered her shoulder, squeezing it gently. "My Katie-bug. Are you sure you're okay?"

"Yes, Dad. I'm fine."

"Everyone's been calling. The entire town knows about the kidnapping and rescue already. They're so concerned about you and Kurtis."

"Nothing stays a secret for very long in Lobster Cove."

"They're worried about you. Linda, Helen, Calla, and even Father Zack called to see how you were doing—they wanted to make sure you and Kurtis had been rescued. Father Zack assured us God would work miracles to find you both safe."

"Let them all know I'm going to be fine."

"We'll have her checked out in a jiffy," the orderly said. "If you'll excuse us, now, Dr. Willson is waiting for Miss Sullivan."

Her mother clung to her hand as she was taken to a glassed-in cubicle, and only then did she let go and step back while Katelyn was transferred to an examination table. A nurse's assistant drew the curtain closed for privacy. She heard her mother's sob. Her own insides clenched.

"She'll be good as new in no time, Dawn. Our baby will be okay," her father comforted her mother.

Exhausted, Katelyn wanted to sleep forever. She lay back, shut her eyes only to have Tracy Novak, an ER nurse, wrap a blood pressure cuff on her arm.

"How you doing, Katelyn? You look like a Mack truck ran you over. How'd you get those bruises?" Tracy rubbed a newfangled thermometer across her forehead, while another medical assistant entered and covered her with a heated blanket.

"Thrown from a van. Road was pretty solid. My

whole body aches, especially my wrist." Not to mention her heart. The heated blanket was bliss.

"We'll check it out. Make sure you're good to go before we release you. I see Mark came to your rescue. He's even more handsome now than he was in high school." Tracy pasted electrode pads all over her chest for an EKG to observe her heart. She lost track of time as Tracy continued to talk and monitor everything connected to her sore body. Her mind floated back to the kidnapping—glad Kurtis was safe, her parents were there, and Mark had rescued her.

Half an hour later, Mark was by her side, waking her with a kiss.

"How are you doing?" He slipped her hand in his and squeezed it. "I'm so sorry this happened to you."

Her eyes fluttered open. She was thirsty, but managed a weak "How is Kurtis? Is he okay?"

"Yes. My parents took him home. They've had undercover round-the-clock security at the house since I arrived—as a precautionary measure to make sure he was safe. It was the only way I could leave his side without worrying 24/7."

"What about when he was at daycare?"

He smiled and she had her answer. He'd had that covered, too.

"I take it you know Gerald Wolfe and Peter Gray?"

"Undercover?"

"Yep. Gerald will be moving on in six months. I'll be taking his place."

"So, you'll be staying in Lobster Cove?"

"It's where I belong. Listen, Katie, I'm really sorry about all this. I didn't think the kidnappers would follow us to Lobster Cove. Thank God my team in

Maine had everything in place and they were able to apprehend those responsible before they got very far. And thanks to Connie for alerting us so quickly that the two of you had been forcibly taken and thrown in a van."

She squeezed his hand still holding hers.

"Are they okay—Connie and Jason?"

"Yes. The kidnappers didn't see them. They were too busy trying to get to Kurtis."

"I'm glad they'll be okay."

"I have to go to a debriefing in a few minutes, but your parents are still here and will take you home. I'll stop by later to make sure you're okay."

He kissed her on the lips, which did more to warm her insides than the heated blanket. He squeezed her hand again, looked at their linked fingers for several seconds before letting go, his flushed face thoughtful. What was he thinking? Was this his way of saying goodbye? Again?

He disappeared around the curtain, the imprint of his kiss lingered in his wake.

****

Mark nodded to the guard outside the cubicle, and then approached Katelyn's parents.

"I assured Katie you'd take her home when they discharge her."

"Is she going to be okay?" Dawn Sullivan clutched her husband's arm.

"Yes. They assured me she is in excellent shape. A bit bruised, a sprained wrist, but no internal bleeding, concussion, frostbite, or hypothermia. Just shaken up a bit. I can't tell you how sorry I am she was involved."

"It's not your fault, son. We're just thankful Kurtis

and Katelyn are safe now. You played a big part in that. We can't thank you enough for finding her before something bad happened."

"Mr. and Mrs. Sullivan, you can see Katelyn now." Tracy stuck her head outside the exam room. "We'll be releasing her as soon as Dr. Willson signs off. It might take a while. He's had another emergency come in."

"If you'll excuse me, I need to meet with the security team." Mark nodded to the Sullivans. "I told Katie I'd stop by later to see how she's doing."

****

Ten minutes later, Mark met with Police Chief Johnson, Gerald Wolfe, Jake MacKenzie, Calla Hutchins, and a few others he hadn't been introduced to, yet.

"You left Bar Harbor just in time." Calla was the first to speak. "The yacht blew up seconds after our men backed off the vessel. One of the Coast Guards got a tip that it was ready to explode once they were out to sea. With all the commotion, I assume they decided not to wait."

Had they planned to blow up the ship with Kurtis on board? Had the mission gone that bad? Shell-shocked at how close he'd come to losing his son, Mark sat, speechless. He rubbed his hands over his face, around his neck, stretched, and sat up straight.

"We apprehended Dimitri Anast Dobromir, a Russian Slovak; Bartosz Carneg from Slovakia; and a Polish national named Jedrek Jearoslav, before they boarded the vessel," Gerald informed him. "Apparently, they had no idea they were going to be blown up along with the yacht. It wasn't hard to encourage them to talk—they were more than willing to spill their guts after watching the explosion."

"Seems you were right," Peter Gray said. "Natasha's parents wanted the boy, afraid you wouldn't allow them access to him. However, the miscreants they hired to kidnap him decided to raise the stakes. They wanted more money. And they hadn't counted on the thugs they hired to be members of the terrorist group we've been following the last three years."

"The entire plot is so screwed up," Jake MacKenzie chimed in, a snicker escaping. "Their right hand didn't know what their left hand was doing, as usual. Thanks to your input, we were able to work together and wrap things up quickly."

"I only met Natasha's parents once—at the wedding. If they'd only talked to me, we could have worked something out."

"I wouldn't worry about that now. The two have been under surveillance by their own government. They were apprehended two days ago. I don't think you're going to hear from them again."

Relief washed over him. As a precautionary measure, he wasn't about to release the two undercover agents watching his family—and Katie—just yet.

Katie. God. He had to go to her—talk to her. It hadn't escaped his notice that her engagement ring was missing from her finger. Had she lost her ring when she'd been tossed out of the van? Had it slipped off her frozen fingers? Or was she no longer engaged to that Sven fellow? He sure as hell was going to find out. But dammit, it was Christmas Eve day. With all that had happened to Kurtis, his son needed something special to celebrate Christmas, to erase the nightmare he'd just gone through. Something memorable. His son deserved special and happy memories. But what would it take to put a smile back on Kurtis' face?

Mark passed the central square, now devoid of all the merriment that had taken place the previous night. How many were aware of the kidnapping? Decorations held a lonely, forlorn, yet peaceful and serene ambiance to the area this morning. His heart was still weighted down with the aftereffects of the kidnapping, and the turmoil he'd caused the people of Lobster Cove. He'd put his family, and Katie, in harm's way. He'd told Katie he was here to stay, but maybe he should think about moving on. He couldn't stand it if something happened to her—again.

The sun rose over the bay, outlining a clear blue sky on the horizon as he pulled in the driveway to his family home. He parked, got out, and rushed up the front steps. His father met him at the door.

"Is everything okay, son? How's Katie?"

"She's going to be fine. They'll release her soon. Dawn and Roark are there with her now, and will take her home when she's released. I'll check in with her later, but I want to make sure Kurtis is doing okay."

"He's two," his father said. "He's taken it like a champ. Takes after his father. Hasn't stopped talking about finding Katie. In his mind, the whole event is like a great adventure—you and he are the heroes. What happened, son? I know you've been uptight since you came home, expecting something like this to take place. Is it over, now?"

"Yes. It's over. I talked to the authorities after I left the hospital." He gave his father a brief rundown of what took place, and why.

"Where is Kurtis, now?" Mark asked, heading for

the kitchen and a cup of coffee.

"In the kitchen with your mother. She's making him pancakes with blueberries and some of this season's maple syrup."

"Sounds good. I could use some breakfast, too."

He found Kurtis tucking in to a large pancake topped with whipped cream. Maple syrup dripped down his chin.

"How you doing, bud." He ruffled Kurtis' hair, and then took a seat beside him. His mother set a plateful of pancakes in front of him. "Thanks. They smell delicious."

"Santa comes tonight," Kurtis said, chewing around a mouthful.

"Don't talk with food in your mouth." He filled his own mouth with breakfast, and then followed it down with coffee, then answered his son. "Yep. Tonight's the night. What'd you ask Santa to bring you?"

"I can't tell. Only Santa knows. He'll bring it, too."

He was well aware what his son wanted for Christmas. He planned to make a few phone calls and make sure he got it. If not today or tomorrow, soon.

"I have to go out for a while after breakfast. You gonna be okay here with Grandma and Grandpa?"

"He's pretty tired, Mark. I think he needs a nap, and then we'll make some cookies. I said I'd provide a couple dozen for coffee after Midnight Mass tonight. Are you coming with us?"

"I plan on it."

They finished breakfast in silence. Mark waited until Kurtis put the last morsel in his mouth, and washed it down with milk.

"Come on, bud. I'll get you settled in for a quick

nap. I'll be back before you know it." After tucking him in bed, he pulled the covers over Kurtis' shoulders, and kissed his forehead. He ruffled his hair again, and then returned to the kitchen. His heart was a bit lighter even though he had a lot to make up for.

"Kurtis' eyes were drooping before I left his room," he told his parents. "I'll be back in a couple hours—I'm going to Katie's, see how she's doing."

"Give her our love," his mother called as he went out the front door.

****

Katelyn answered the door before he could knock twice. Her red reindeer jogging pants and green sweatshirt made her look like she did back in high school. He stepped back long enough to shut the door, then lifted her in his arms. He carried her to the living room, sat on the sofa and nestled her in his lap. She snuggled into his shoulder.

"You're safe now, sweetheart. Everything is going to be okay. I promise."

She sighed against his chest—his insides tightened as her essence surrounded him—her bath soap, apple scented shampoo were a heady elixir. The fireplace was alight, glittering off the decorations on the tree. She'd put Christmas music on, and it was playing soft and low. God, he wanted her to stay in his arms like this, forever. He shut his eyes wondering how he could make things right for her.

"I'm so sorry, Katie." He kissed her hair, ran his fingers through the silken strands. "So sorry you got involved in this ugly mess. I should never have come back home and put you in danger. This is all my fault. And God only knows I could never live with myself if

I'd lost both you and Kurtis."

He lifted her face to his and kissed her. She wound her arms around his neck and clung to him. The kiss continued, he lost any semblance of control, and laid her back on the sofa. Damn! She was still cold and half frozen. And bruised. He slid his hands down her arm, covered her hip.

"God, Katie, you feel so good, I want to make love to you, but I'm afraid I'll hurt you—you must be hurting like hell."

"Right now I don't feel a single ache or pain."

"I've wanted to make love to you since I returned home. Since I saw you in that sexy elf outfit. You had my heart beating triple time."

"I looked like a clown. I was so mortified when I realized you were Santa."

"Definitely not a clown. I couldn't take my eyes off you."

He ran his hands over her spine, and then wrapped them around her buttocks, pulling her tighter. Her hands slipped below and found his tight butt cheeks, returning the favor—his erection gave his wishes away. He wanted, needed, to make love to her so bad, he had all to do to hold back to make sure she wanted this as much as he did.

Did she want to make love with Mark? Hell, yes. She didn't care whether it was the right thing to do or not. She had wanted him for so long, and darn it, she was in his arms, and she wasn't about to let this chance slip away—bruises or no bruises.

His hand slipped under her shirt and circled her breast—her bones turned to mush.

"Mark?"

"Hush, let me love you."

"Yes, please."

He snatched the quilt from the sofa and carried it, and her, to the rug in front of the fireplace. Her sweater flew over her head, her sweatpants magically slid down her legs. She kicked them to the side. It didn't take long for Mark to lose his clothes, as well. He took her in his arms and together they sank to the floor, the quilt forgotten as their bodies connected—skin to skin, heartbeat to heartbeat, lips to lips. His hands cupped her face, bringing her lips to fit his—the kiss was dynamite—her insides burst with need that she'd been craving for so long. Not missing a single beat, Katelyn wrapped her arms around Mark, arched into his hold in invitation. He didn't hesitate. His hands slid along her ribcage, over her hips and down her thighs. The heat from those magical hands consumed her. She was in heaven, her body turned to molten lava—she was ready to burst. She ran her hands along his muscular biceps, over his shoulders, and then massaged her fingers along his spine to the dip just above his ass. She splayed her hands over his very tight buns and pulled him to her, his erection snuggled between her legs.

"Oh, God, Katie. You don't know what you're doing to me. I don't think I can wait much longer to be inside you. To make love to you."

"Mmmm. No talk. Just love me."

He let her go and she felt the cold between their bodies like a dash of icy water. She stiffened. What the…?

"My jeans? Where are my jeans?"

"What? What'd I say? Why are you leaving?"

"No, no. I'm not leaving, sweetheart. I'm looking

for my jeans—I brought protection."

Katelyn relaxed, glad he found his jeans in record time, pulled the small packet from the front pocket, ripped it open with his teeth, and was shielded in seconds. He covered her body with his, and together they rekindled their lost love.

Much later, spent, and in Mark's arms, Katelyn rested, spoon fashion, against him, his arms pulled her into his strong, warm body. They lay quietly for long moments, sated, complete.

"I'm so sorry for walking out on you the other night, Katie. I don't know what got into me. I was angry with myself, not you. I hated that you went through a miscarriage without me. Just thinking of the pain and anguish you must have suffered, alone. And it was my fault. The fact that I didn't know about any of it made me feel like I had no control—that I was left out of a big part of what we had together. You do understand that if I had been aware of your pregnancy I would have been there in a heartbeat?"

"Maybe that's why I didn't try so hard to find you. I didn't want you to give up everything you'd worked so hard for. I didn't want you to grow to hate me, being tied to me, especially after I lost the baby."

"Will you...that is...."

"Yes, I'll still be able to have children." She ran her good hand over his cheek, the soft stubble of his ten o'clock shadow was like a caress on her fingertips.

"I'm glad." He hugged her, and she nestled closer, if that was possible. She was in his arms, and that was something to be grateful for.

"I could never hate you. *Never*." He took her left hand in his and rubbed his thumb over her fingers. "I hope this mean you are no longer engaged."

She turned in his arms and wound her arms around his neck, her breasts brushing up against his strong chest. "I'm no longer engaged. Going to Norway was a big mistake—sort of. Apparently Sven got engaged to an old girlfriend while he was there, and didn't know how to tell me."

"I'm so sorry you had to go through that, too." He kissed her forehead.

Katie sighed, and then continued, "It explained a lot. He'd been hedging every time I talked about setting a date. And honestly, once you came back to Lobster Cove and started kissing me, I realized I'd never gotten over you. I don't blame Sven for the breakup—he did us both a favor—I know now we never truly loved each other. I just wish he'd had the guts to break up with me before I flew half a world away only to make a fool of myself."

She lay quietly in his arms, cuddling. He wrapped the blanket around them, sighed, and rested his chin on her head.

"You're no fool, sweetheart. He is. But I'm glad he broke it off. Although I didn't love Natasha either, I don't regret my short time with her—she did give me Kurtis."

"What about you and Connie?"

"What about me and Connie?"

"Weren't you two a couple?"

"What? No, of course not."

"It looked like you two were a couple."

"Jason and Kurtis are friends. We arranged play dates—I had to be there to protect my son. Connie's husband and I played ball back in high school—I was sorry to hear about his death."

"Yes, so was I. I've seen how hard it's been on her."

"Exactly. I know what it's like being a single parent. Don't tell me you were jealous?"

"No. Not really…well, maybe a little."

"Nothing to worry about. We're just friends. I swear."

He nudged her chin toward his lips, the kiss igniting a spark, which to her delight, led to another round of exquisite lovemaking.

Chapter Fourteen

Their lingering kiss had his mind and body wanting more. Much more. But he had to leave.

"I hate to go, Katie, but I promised Kurtis I'd take him to pick up a special Christmas present this afternoon. Something I hope will help take his mind off the kidnapping. I've made arrangements to be there no later than one o'clock." He rubbed his hands along her arms—not wanting to leave. "I don't want to be late."

"I'm sure he'll love whatever you've decided to give him. Is it a puppy? I know he wants a puppy, but that's not always a good idea. It's a huge responsibility for a little guy."

"He's a trouper and deserves something special. I wasn't ready for a dog so soon, either, but my folks agreed it was a great idea, especially after everything Kurtis has been through tonight."

"Oh, Mark. You're really going to get him a puppy? He'll be over the moon."

"How about you go with us? You can play elf."

"You're never going to let me forget this elf thing, are you?" She smiled, getting used to his teasing.

"It was the best homecoming gift a man could ask for. What do you say? Come with us. Kurtis will be thrilled to have you come along. That's all Kurtis has been asking for since he spotted that one at the Scout's tree stand."

"I remember. It was so cute romping around the trees in the snow. Oh, my goodness, Mark, Kurtis is going to love you forever. Yes, I'd love to come. I can't wait to see his face when he picks out his puppy. He'd been hugging that book on dogs at daycare every chance he got. That's all he's talked about. So where did you find someone willing to part with a dog today, of all days?"

"Doc Weaver at the Old Mill Vets told me about an elderly couple in Ellsworth. Billis...Bilton...something like that..."

"Bilson—Henry and Ramona Bilson?"

"Yes. That's them. Anyway, their dog just had a litter a few months ago. They only have three pups left. I gave them a call, told them what I was looking for and why, and they insisted I come by today so Kurtis could take his pick of the litter in time for Christmas."

"I know the Bilsons. They're frequent visitors to Mariner's Fish Fry when they come to town. I didn't know they had a black lab. I'm not surprised they were willing to have you stop by the day before Christmas. They're such a pleasant, caring couple." And this was something they wouldn't hesitate to do, regardless of their own Christmas schedule. The world needed more people like them.

Mark pulled the blanket around her, kissed her bare shoulder, than pulled her with him as they sat up. "How about I let you get dressed while I pick up Kurtis, then I'll swing back around to get you in a half hour."

He loved the way Katie blushed—if it weren't for the quilt, he'd swear her entire naked body warmed clear to her toes. Clinging to the blanket did nothing to hide the vision of them making love next to the fire moments ago. If he read the look in her eyes correctly, she didn't want him to leave either. He leaned in, kissed her, stepped away, and turned the door handle.

"I'll be back soon."

God, it killed him to shut the door on her when all he wanted to do was take her in his arms again, and make love to her one more time. If it weren't for his promise to Kurtis, that's exactly what he'd be doing.

The afternoon sun was bright, the winter sky an azure blue—euphoria filled his entire being. Who knew a simple winter's day in coastal Maine could add a lift to his heavy heart. Of course, his love for Katie was stronger than ever and might have something to do with it, that and having made mad passionate love to her. He was never going to let her go again.

****

Katelyn made her way to the bedroom. If she hurried, she could get in a quick shower before Mark and Kurtis returned. She couldn't think of a better way to spend the day before Christmas than with Mark and Kurtis. This was turning out to be her best Christmas ever. Being held in Mark's strong arms, making love with him, and hearing him tell her he loved her, was the best Christmas present. Especially after her disastrous weekend in Norway, and thinking there was no hope in hell of finding a true love. It didn't matter that there had been no promises made, no commitments from Mark. The chance to build on their renewed love was a start. They'd both been through a lot during their separation—she vowed to help him rebuild his life here in Lobster Cove—his and Kurtis'.

She quickly showered, dressed in jeans, a blue fuzzy sweater, her black boots, and matching scarf, hat and gloves. She was ready in record time, waiting when Mark drew the car to a stop in her driveway. Before he could get out, and meet her at the door, Katelyn rushed down the sidewalk. He met her at the car with open arms, kissed her, escorted her to the passenger side, and opened the door.

"Hi, Kurtis. Merry Christmas," she called over her shoulder, then turned back around and buckled her seat belt.

Mark slid in across from her and put the car in reverse.

"Merry Christmas, Katie. I'm gonna get a puppy. Santa told Daddy to get me one." He giggled and clapped his hands.

"I heard. You must be thrilled."

The excitement in Kurtis' voice was music to her ears. Mark was right. He couldn't have chosen a better gift for his son. Kids were certainly more resilient than adults. It was going to take her more than a puppy to get over the effects of being kidnapped and dumped along the road in the middle of the night, in freezing temperatures.

Kurtis talked nonstop about black lab puppies on the way to the Bilsons' as if he was already an expert on the care and feeding of the breed. His excitement renewed her own spirits, and before she realized it, they were off the island and entering Ellsworth. The Bilsons met them at the door, welcoming them with waving hands and warm smiles the minute they spotted Kurtis.

"What a handsome young man." Mrs. Bilson clapped her hands together. "Why, this is going to be perfect. Just perfect. Don't you think so, Henry?"

"Absolutely, my dear. And Katelyn. What a

surprise. How nice to see you, too."

"Hi, Mr. and Mrs. Bilson. This is Mark and Kurtis Logan. It's kind of you to let us come today. You must be busy getting ready for your own Christmas."

"Thanks for seeing us on such short notice. It's very kind you," Mark chimed in. "As I said on the phone, this puppy means a lot to Kurtis."

"Not a problem. Come. Come. We've kept the litter in the mudroom off from the kitchen. It's too cold for them outside, and the heat from the kitchen is just the right temperature, and it keeps them out from under foot." Mr. Bilson led them around the side of the house. "They're starting to be a real handful, so it's time to let them go. There are three left. You can take your pick, young man."

Henry opened the door to the mudroom, a disheveled wad of material used as bedding lay in the corner, next to a washer and dryer. Several size dog dishes were scattered about the floor. As soon as Kurtis stepped inside, three small black lab puppies started barking in unison, wagged their tails, and tripped over themselves to get to him. Kurtis kneeled, opened his arms, and welcomed all three hyper pups.

"Puppies. Daddy. Look, puppies. Just what I asked Santa to bring me."

"That's right, bud. Go ahead and pick out the one you like. Santa told me the Bilsons were the ones to contact for your Christmas present. He wanted you to pick out just the right one."

Kurtis laughed as the puppies continued to vie for his attention. They jumped up on him, circled around him, licked his face and hands, and nipped at his ears. One finally jumped up into his lap, curled up and put his head on his paws, his eyes darting back and forth at the adults. Kurtis hugged the pup to his small body. The dog stretched up and leaned his furry face into Kurtis' neck and stayed there—both content to be in each other's arms.

"I think Kurtis has made a decision—or at least the puppy has chosen Kurtis." Mark smiled.

Katie ran her hand over the puppy's soft furry head. The dog's eyes looked into hers, then back at Kurtis, and licked his cheek as if to say it was where he belonged.

"What's his name?" Kurtis asked.

"Well, now, that's up to you, young man. Do you have a name picked out?" Mr. Bilson asked.

Kurtis looked to his father. "Your choice, bud." Mark assured him. "You don't have to decide right this minute. Take your time."

"Can I call her Tasha?"

Kurtis might be too young to remember his mother, but he hadn't forgotten he had one, or that her name was Natasha. She watched Kurtis stroke the puppy's furry head, run his hand along its back. Katelyn was overcome with longing, wanting to take both of them in her arms and hug them close. Mark and his parents were right. This was exactly what Mark's son needed. The dog licked Kurtis' cheek again.

"Tasha, it is," Mark said.

Katelyn turned so the others wouldn't see her wipe a stray tear from her face.

"If you know of anyone else looking for a pup or two, send them our way," Mr. Bilson chuckled.

"We will. Thanks again for letting us impose during your holiday."

"Think nothing of it. So glad we could help make your Christmas a merry one. You take care."

Back in the car, Kurtis didn't let go of the puppy—he held Tasha in his lap, the puppy content to be held, petted, and talked to during the entire trip home.

"I'm sorry about the dog's name," Mark said, for Katelyn's ears only. He backed the car up, then turned and drove out of the Bilson's driveway, and headed toward Lobster Cove.

"Don't be. I think it's wonderful he wants to honor his mother's memory this way. Even if he doesn't remember her, it's admirable for a boy so young to be so thoughtful. You've done an amazing job raising him, Mark. You should be proud."

"Thanks. I don't want the mention of her name on a daily basis to come between us." He took her hand in his and squeezed it gently. "I messed up, Katie, but I aim to rectify that if you'll let me. I want us to start over…to be together again."

"I'd like that, too." She squeezed his hand in return, their fingers twining.

"We're going to Midnight Mass at St. Joe's tonight. Come with me."

"It's been our family tradition since I was a little girl."

"We'll all go together, then. I'll pick you up—we can meet the parents at the church."

****

Strains of "O Come All Ye Faithful" filled the church as parishioners flocked to Midnight Mass. Katelyn was greeted with hugs and well wishes for the speedy rescue and a full recovery by several of her friends and older parishioners she'd known all her life.

Their concern was endearing. No one seemed surprised to see her with Mark and Kurtis. In fact, everyone fussed over Kurtis to the point that he tunneled his head in Mark's neck from all the attention. It felt a bit awkward walking down the aisle to Mark's family pew instead of their usual seat, but Mark kept one arm around her waist while holding Kurtis in the other. Kurtis snuggled in between them when they sat.

Despite everyone's blasé acceptance of them arriving as a couple, Katelyn knew Lobster Cove's rumor mill was going to be heating up after tonight. It didn't go unnoticed, however, that no one had bothered to ask about Sven—or why she was with Mark. She didn't care—it would be a seven-day wonder, and the rumor mill would soon pounce on the next Lobster Cove incident.

Katelyn had trouble concentrating on the service, even though she knew it by rote. She stood, kneeled, sang, crossed herself numerous times, and gave thanks for the safe rescue of Kurtis, and herself. While she was at it, she gave thanks for bringing Mark back home, safe and sound, to Lobster Cove. To her.

The jubilation of Christmas filled the church. Overwhelmed, she looked around at the congregation with a sense of pride and well-being—she couldn't envision a more caring community in which to live.

A moment of peaceful silence filled the church once the service ended. The organ suddenly struck a chord, and the choir joined in with "Joy to the World," bells rang in the background as everyone stood to leave. Mark ushered her from the church, his arm around her, his hand squeezing her hip, while he held a sleepy boy in his other arm.

Her heart was full to overflowing.

"I'm going to take Katie home, bud," he whispered in his son's ear. By the time they reached the car, a light snow had begun to fall, the hush of it magical as it surrounded them in the quiet night. "You go with Grandma and Grandpa—they'll help you put milk and cookies on the table for Santa. Make sure Tasha is settled for the night before Grandma tucks you in bed. I'll check on you when I get home."

"Night, Katie."

"Goodnight, Kurtis." Katelyn leaned in and kissed his cheek, her heart full of love. "Merry Christmas, sweetie."

"Want to come in?" Katelyn asked as soon as Mark pulled into the drive and shut the engine off.

"I thought you'd never ask." He leaned over and kissed her cheek.

Katelyn smiled and opened the door to get out, only to have Mark by her side in seconds. He swooped her into his arms and carried her inside. Boots, winter coats, hats, scarves, and gloves littered the floor, missing the nearest chair as they made it to the hearth in record time.

"My favorite spot." He nuzzled her neck as he laid her down on the throw rug. "Why isn't the fire going?"

"I never leave it on while I'm away from home."

"No problem, sweetheart, there's plenty of fire inside me right now to keep us both warm all night long. Come here, Elf, and let me prove it you."

He kissed her lips, deepened the embrace. She twined her arms around his neck and drew him in closer. She'd been beside herself with longing all the while they'd sat together in church. His kisses curled her toes, but that wasn't enough. She wanted more—so much more. She wanted Mark. Forever. For always.

She sent up another silent prayer of thanks for sending Mark back to her.

"Oh, God, Katie," he moaned. "I love you so much. I just about freaked when I heard you'd been kidnapped along with Kurtis."

"I love you, too, Mark. I haven't stopped loving you."

"I'm so sorry…"

"Hush, it's all in the past. We're together now."

"You're too forgiving."

"So I've been told a few times. But I'm serious—we've found each other again and that's all that matters."

"God, I love you. You will marry me, won't you? I'm not about to let you get out of my sight again."

"Oh, Mark. Yes. Yes, I'll marry you. But what about Kurtis? Do you think he'll mind? He's been through so much already. You don't think this will be another hurdle he'll have to deal with, do you? A new mother? And after just naming his puppy after his biological mother?"

He brushed her hair behind her ears, and gazed into her eyes.

"Kurtis adjusts better than any adult I know. To make sure he's adjusting to all these changes, I've had him evaluated by a child's advocacy group. He has another appointment scheduled for the first of the year to make sure the trauma of this kidnapping episode hasn't left him badly scarred. With the puppy and having you for a mother—he loves you already, by the way—I think he's going to be just fine."

His kiss melted her bones, her body turned to liquid in his arms.

Oh, my God! Kurtis' mother! The notion that she would raise Mark's son as her own caught her off-guard. A tear slipped from her eyes. Mark caught it with his lips, kissed it away.

"Oh, Katie. Come here." He tightened his hold on her. "I didn't mean to spring this on you so soon. Especially after all you've been through—the miscarriage, the kidnapping. This must be disconcerting. I'm didn't mean to be so insensitive. I'm sorry."

"Mark. I'm okay. Really. I'm just a bit emotional because I'd love to be Kurtis' mother. The fact that you want me to be his mother is such a gift of love, I'm ecstatic—these are tears of joy."

Mark tucked her in his arms, leaving a trail of sensual kisses from behind her ear, to her neckline. His teeth tugged at her sweater's fuzzy fabric.

"We need to remove this before I do it damage."

"Not a problem. But you'll have to return the favor. It's getting very hot in here."

"Say no more."

They made love, lay in each other's arms through the night, and then made love again—and slept. Mark woke in the early hours, rose on his elbow, and watched Katie sleep. He brushed his hand over her smooth, rosy cheeks, and listened to her breathe—her chest rising and falling in a steady rhythm. He loved her, loved the way she had made love to him without reserve, how she cuddled against him all night. He couldn't wait until they were married and he wouldn't have to leave her bed, ever again. He thanked God for his supreme powers in bringing them back together—for keeping his Katie safe.

He leaned over and kissed her softly on the lips. God, it was going to kill him to have to leave her so soon after finding paradise in her arms. If it wasn't for having to be with Kurtis when he woke to discover the presents Santa had left under the tree, he'd crawl right back in Katie's bed and make love to her one more time.

He couldn't help himself, he kissed her again, and whispered in her ear. "Katie, love, I hate to leave, but I have to go home and be there when Kurtis wakes."

She wrapped her arms around his neck, arched up to meet him, and snuggled into him—God, he was lost. Her soft warmth encompassed him. He inched the covers aside, lay beside her and buried his face in her luscious, thick, silky hair, breathing in her scent. He pulled her naked body on top of him, the ache between his legs heavy. God help him, he wanted to be inside her one more time. He groaned when she nibbled on his neck and then traced her tongue down over his nipple. He lifted her, gained easy access to her plush breasts and returned the favor. When he'd had his fill, and neither of them could wait any longer, he rolled over, taking her with him. He almost lost it when she wrapped her legs around him and urged him inside her—to make love to her. *Ahh, no words were necessary. Her wish was his command.*

Much later, as much as he wanted to lie in bed with her all day, he had to leave or he wasn't going to make it home in time to watch Kurtis open his gifts from Santa. He nudged her shoulder, sorry to wake her. "I'll be back soon, sweetheart. How about having breakfast with Santa later this morning?"

She stretched, sat up, pulled the covers around her shoulders, and yawned.

"As long as I don't have to wear that ridiculous—"

"Sexy!"

"Ridiculous elf outfit."

"Actually, you're looking sexier without anything on. I wish I could stay longer, sweetheart, but I gotta go."

"You don't look too bad au naturel, yourself, Santa. Are you sure you can't stay longer?"

"I really should be going." He kissed her forehead. "I'll see you later."

Mark left Katelyn snuggled in bed as he contemplated his many blessings. Santa certainly had given him the best Christmas present a man could ask for—a Christmas to remember.

****

Katelyn anticipated the knock on the door later that morning. The coffee, hot cocoa, pancake batter and blueberries at the ready, she flew to the entrance to welcome Mark and Kurtis. She laughed when she saw their red and white matching Santa hats, the white tassels flopping to the side. Before she could comment, Mark wrapped her in his arms, and kissed her—long and hard. She didn't resist, this time.

"Merry Christmas, Katie," Kurtis said, his smile contagious.

"Merry Christmas, Kurtis. What have you got there?"

He handed her a green felt cap. "Daddy said this is for you. Like the one you wore at the Christmas party."

She looked at Mark, and couldn't resist his smile,

and that sexy dimple. Who was she to dispute his idea of what a sexy elf looked like? She couldn't contain the bubbly emotions swelling inside. Her happiness knew no end.

"Why, thank you, Kurtis." She took the cap from him and put it on her head. "There, how does that look?"

"Perfect." Mark reached outside the door and produced a small brown sack.

"What's that?" she asked.

"What's a Santa without presents to put under the tree, right, bud?"

"We brought presents." He clapped his hands.

"I think the real Santa left some presents for you here, as well." Katie took Kurtis' hand. "Let's go see what's under the tree."

Mark put the sack on the floor and pulled her into his arms for another hungry kiss while Kurtis knelt down and proceeded to pull the gifts out of the sack and place them under the tree next to the ones Katie had wrapped before going to Midnight Mass.

"Before we open presents"—Mark knelt next to Kurtis, the two of them facing her—"we have something to ask you, don't we, bud?"

"Yes. We want you to marry us and be my mommy." He held out a small black jeweler's box. The look of anticipation as he waited for her answer struck her speechless.

"You were supposed to wait for me, bud." Mark told his son, never breaking eye contact with her. "Well, Katie, what do you say?"

"Yes, Kurtis, I'd love to be your mother, if that's what you really want."

Kurtis ran to her. She enveloped him in her arms, as tears of joy filled her eyes. She looked at Mark and noticed his eyes weren't exactly dry, either. He joined them, and the three of them wound their arms around each other in a group hug. She felt the kiss Mark placed on the top of her head at the same time Kurtis kissed her cheek. Her insides melted.

"Are we a family now, Daddy? Am I gonna have a mommy again?"

"Yep, we're a family, bud. Katie is going to be your mommy."

Katelyn sighed. A family of her own. Definitely the very best Christmas ever.